# ALPHA'S WAR

RENEE ROSE
LEE SAVINO

**Copyright © May 2018 Alpha's War by Renee Rose and Lee Savino**

All rights reserved. This copy is intended for the original purchaser of this book ONLY. No part of this book may be reproduced, scanned, or distributed in any printed or electronic form without prior written permission from the authors. Please do not participate in or encourage piracy of copyrighted materials in violation of the authors' rights. Purchase only authorized editions.

Published in the United States of America

Renee Rose Romance, Silverwood Press and Midnight Romance, LLC

Editor: MJ

This book is a work of fiction. While reference might be made to actual historical events or existing locations, the names, characters, places and incidents are either the product of the authors' imaginations or are used fictitiously, and any resemblance to actual persons, living or dead, business establishments, events, or locales is entirely coincidental.

This book contains descriptions of many BDSM and sexual practices, but this is a work of fiction and, as such, should not be used in any way as a guide. The author and publisher will not be responsible for any loss, harm, injury, or death resulting from use of the information contained within. In other words, don't try this at home, folks!

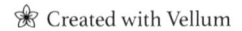

❦ Created with Vellum

## WANT FREE BOOKS?

**-Go to http://subscribepage.com/alphastemp** to sign up for Renee Rose's newsletter and receive a free copy of *Alpha's Temptation, Theirs to Protect, Owned by the Marine, Theirs to Punish, The Alpha's Punishment, Disobedience at the Dressmaker's* and *Her Billionaire Boss*. In addition to the free stories, you will also get special pricing, exclusive previews and news of new releases.

-Go to www.leesavino.com to sign up for Lee Savino's awesomesauce mailing list and get a FREE Berserker book —too hot to publish anywhere else!

# 1

## Denali

I STILL DREAM of him at night.

The deep rasp of his voice. The sense of quiet command, even as a prisoner. The giant bulge of his muscles when he moved. When he shook and sweat above me, his thick manhood filling me, satisfying me.

Sometimes I swear I feel the gentleness of his touch just before I wake. But then I always hear the nightmare voice. The rough snarl of a lion in pain.

*Denali, I'm coming for you.*

I bolt upright in bed, gasping. Just a dream. *A dream, a dream, a dream, a dream.* Another dream.

Not real.

It doesn't take a psychotherapist to know what the dream means.

I shove back the memories of the lion who marked me, ignoring the familiar twist in the pit of my stomach.

Nash.

Did he ever make it out? Or did he die in there and it's his ghost who visits me in the night?

Will the guilt over not going back to try to save him ever run dry? Doubtful.

I throw off the covers and pad silently to the kitchen, careful not to make any noise to wake Nolan.

I make coffee and wave through the window at my portly neighbor and landlady, Mrs. Davenfield, who is out early weeding her garden. She's the reason I ended up settling here.

After I escaped, I stayed off the radar. Took only under the table cash jobs—gardening and migrant farm work. I ended up in Temecula—wine country—working the vineyards during harvest season.

Mrs. Davenfield was willing to take cash and skip the credit check to let me rent the little cottage on her property. She took one look at my swollen belly and decided I must be escaping domestic abuse. I never corrected her, because hell, she seems to love the drama and feeling like she's my secret-keeper. And I needed her help.

And in a way, I was escaping domestic abuse. Just not the way she imagined it. Not some baby-daddy I had to get away from.

No. Nolan's father is the only part of my horrifying ordeal worth remembering. I guess that's why he's the one who haunts me most.

Because I got away.

And I left him there to rot.

∼

## Nash

*Cold light. Grey light. The howls rise in my ears.*

*The concrete walls never change, but at night, they close in. My lion can see in the dark but that doesn't mean night doesn't affect me. I always know when it falls.*

*And those howls.*

*I don't know whether they're real or imagined. I've killed so many. Their screams are my penance. Awake or dreaming, it's all the same. My life is the nightmare that never ends.*

Someone, somewhere is singing.

"When Irish eyes are smiling..."

Barred sunlight trickles over my face. I'm in bed, not a cot. The walls are no longer concrete but dingy white. And paper thin. I hear voices murmuring in the living room, along with the Irish caterwauling. The sound washes over me, and my knotted muscles relax.

My vision, tinged red, clears as my lion retreats. I'm in a bedroom, not a cell with guards outside the door waiting to burst in. But my animal is ready to fight. He always is. Years of abuse have permanently broken him.

Sweat soaks the sheets under me. Another bad night, filled with dreams of being locked in a cell. Or flashbacks. But sometimes, the dreams feel more real.

I pull myself out of bed and make it with military precision, like I have every damn day since week one of bootcamp. "You can take the man out of the army, but not the army out of the man," my drill instructor told us. He was right. But sometimes I wonder if I'll ever be able to take the killer out of my lion.

As soon as I open my bedroom door, the singing stops.

"Nash?" A head pops into the hall.

"What are you doing here?" I glare at the shifter, a young face with a shock of prematurely grey hair.

Parker shrugs and steps back so I can enter the living room. "Got kicked out of my last place. They saw my animal running around and told me *no pets*. And you have an extra room."

I have nothing to say to this, so I turn to the other two interlopers lounging on the battered couch. Two men, one with black hair and a bottle of rotgut in his hands, the other taller than all of us and too thin. The tall one wears thick glasses and blinks constantly. The black haired one grins.

"I told you not to come here," I growl to the room at large.

"You've got the biggest place." Parker hides a smile. For a moment I consider wiping it off his face, then wiping the floor with him. But no. He's my manager. If I fuck him up, who will schedule my fights? Bleeding an opponent on a regular basis is the only thing keeping my animal alive.

"Hey." I point to the black-haired man, who's opening a bottle with an illegible handwritten label. "What the fuck is that stuff? Stinks like paint remover."

"This? Just a wee bit o' hair of the dog. Had a good night last night drinkin' and such. This will perk me up right quick." The Irish accent penetrates, and my brain throws up a name. *Declan.* Shifter—animal unknown. He smells a bit like a wolf, a bit like... something else. A shifter mix, a product of the experiments in the underground labs of Data-X. The Irishman is one of the few that survived. I'd call him lucky, but he's not. The lucky ones died or escaped early. The rest of us still suffer, even though we got away. Even though we burned the place to the ground.

"Ya want some?" Declan offers the bottle. My lion surges to the fore. I beat him back down. As tempting as it is to get drunk before noon, I didn't break out of the prison lab to waste my days.

"No. Drink it outside. Or better yet, use it to kill the grass in the driveway."

"Right ya are, sir." The black-haired man throws off a mock salute. "You're the alpha."

"I'm not your alpha," I call as I head to the kitchen. Breakfast. Food. Normalcy. Go through the motions, even if normal is a foreign country I'll never visit again.

"You're the king of the beasts, aren't ya now? If you're in a pack, you'll be at the lead."

"We're not a pack." I open the fridge and grab the first thing that looks good—a container of milk. I tip it up and drink straight out of the carton, ignoring Parker leaning in the door.

"Ready for the big fight?"

I grunt.

"Another grizzly shifter. This one from Saskatchewan or some Godforsaken place. I swear all they do in the lumber yards is fight."

"Good." Less chance my lion will kill them.

"Betting's pretty evenly split," Parker muses. "The bruins are the only ones who can take you."

A plastic container filled with some sort of homemade biscuits sits on my counter. I tap it. "What's this?"

"Scones. Laurie made them." As soon as he says it I smell the feathery scent of the owl shifter along with the sharp sugary tang of the baked good. I open the container and take two.

My pocket vibrates and pull out my phone. A text from an unknown number.

*Layne and I are driving over. We have intel for you.*

I type back, *I'll be at The Pit.* And because I can't stop myself. *What intel?*

*Kylie got a hit on a woman living in Temecula. Going to confirm now, but we think it's Denali.*

Denali.

*Red. Black. The cell door opens, I stand at ready. The guards come in, weapons trained on me. I expect them.*

*I don't expect her. The scent of cinnamon fills the air. Cinnamon... and arousal.*

"Nash? Nash?"

The memory goes dark, and ebbs away, leaving Parker's worried face. Behind him, Declan and Laurie stand at the door, staring at me.

The world tints red for a second. My lion trying to take hold. These flashbacks are unmanageable. I'm barely sane on a good day. What will happen if it *is* Denali?

"I gotta go." Two steps to the door, and I reverse, grabbing another scone and holding it up for the tall man to see. "Thanks. These are good."

The owl shifter blinks at me from behind his Coke-bottle glasses.

I leave out the back door.

# 2

# N*ash*

This time of day, The Pit is mostly deserted, which is a good thing, my lion is riled up enough at the lingering smell of shifters. I let him out and prowl around the grounds. We're far enough in a run-down industrial district that no one will see a lion pacing the perimeter of a dingy warehouse. No one comes back here but shifters, and the shifters who come here will recognize me. This is my territory. My kingdom. I let my mad lion mark his territory, slinking along the chain link fence that surrounds the parking lot, then I shift and put my clothes back on. I head inside for a drink, trying not to think of how pathetic I've become.

A few minutes later, a blond man steps inside, sniffing the air. At the bar, I raise my glass in invitation. He nods and steps back, allowing his companion to enter before him. A striking, young Asian woman with long dark hair approaches. She stares right at me. I meet her gaze in mild challenge. She's a new shifter—one of the more successful creations of Dr. Smyth's, and dominant. My lion normally would challenge her boldness, but right now he doesn't see her as a threat. This is a meeting of allies, and he knows he's about to get what he wants.

Sam sits. Without a word, he lays his phone on the bar, screen up. There's a picture of a woman leaving a house, her face half shuttered behind the screen door.

My chest tightens. *Denali*. The room blurs, turning red.

Sam puts a finger on the screen and swipes to show me the rest. Denali headed down the drive, entering a car. Long legs in cutoff shorts, a plain white tee showcasing lean taut arms. "My contact took them this morning. Confirmed the address of the house. She seems to be living there." Sam slides a piece of paper to me, but I can't tear my eyes away from the picture. In every photo, there's a serious expression on her face—not quite sad. Distant.

"Is this her?" Layne asks.

"Yes." I find my voice. "It's her." *Denali. Mine,* my lion roars, shaking the bars of his cage. He wants to come out and go on the hunt. Find Denali, make his claim. *Mine.*

Crimson clouds my vision. I blink, and everything goes black.

I raise my head, realizing I've been silent for a few minutes. The air is thick with tension. Layne's eyes are shifter bright. They know I'm unhinged. Hell, I could've killed Sam last year when he decided the best way to enlist my aid in finding Dr. Smyth was to go a round in the ring with me. He brought up Denali and I partially shifted right there in the cage. Put my claws right through him. But he survived, and we got Smyth. And this is what he promised me in return—finding my mate.

"Sorry it took so long," Sam says. The hair on his arms stands on end, but his voice is calm. He might not be the biggest shifter, but he's a cool head under pressure. Unlike the rest of us. "I thought for sure we had her last time."

My fist clenches and I have to work to relax it. "She probably moves around a lot." She'll be hiding like we are. Always looking over her shoulder. Never knowing if someone who wants to do more testing will show up.

"She seems to have settled. The landlady of this place wouldn't say when she moved in or give any information about her." Sam flicks the paper bearing the address. "But we better move fast. Layne and I can—"

"No." I pocket the paper. "Just me. Alone."

"With all due respect—" Sam eases off the barstool a second after me. He doesn't try to get in my way, but he steps too close. Color explodes behind my eyes. Darkness dances at the corners, then takes over.

A second later, I come to. My hands are fisted in Sam's shirt. I've slammed him against the bar. He shows his neck, a wolf's signal of yielding. His hands go up, spread in surrender, but my lion doesn't care. My canines ache as they grow, a growl blasting from my throat.

A second later pain explodes in my back.

"I wouldn't if I were you." A purr in my ear, soft and sibilant. The claws in my skin flex and tighten, ten points of agony, needle sharp. "Be a good kitty and let him go."

Wrenching hold of my lion, I release Sam's shirt, and snarl as the claws bite deeper.

"Layne," Sam murmurs. A half purr, half growl and the weight leaves my back abruptly. I stretch, ignoring the shriek of pain along my spine, and turn slowly. The woman stares straight at me with almond-shaped cat eyes. If she were male, my lion would want to have a round with her, even though I'm the asshole here. But I admire her strength. Her grace. And I appreciate what she and Sam are doing for me.

Still, my lion can't stop me from posturing. "Most wouldn't provoke the king of the beasts in his territory."

Layne meets my challenge with a glare. Sam slips to her side and she takes his hand without breaking her gaze. *Don't threaten my mate,* she seems to say. My lion grudgingly approves.

"Maybe it's best if you do go alone, Nash." Sam tugs Layne to the door.

As soon as they step outside, I cover my face with a hand. My forehead is clammy with effort from keeping my lion on a chain. He's violent, lashing out at friend and foe. I'm dangerous. Desperate. I'm dying, and there's only one cure.

*Denali.*

The paper in my pocket nudges my palm. I crumple it and fight the rising red tide that threatens my vision. It hurts, but I push it back.

"Well, boss? You gonna get her?" Parker stands in front of me.

I didn't realize the gang had followed me to The Pit from my house, but it figures. They're omnipresent. "I can't." I force the words out, ignoring my lion's howl of loss.

"Ya must," Declan says at my side. "Your lion can't hold on any longer."

"I know." I close my eyes. I was supposed to find Denali, go to her. Apologize. Make sure she's safe.

It's too late. My lion is out of control, and I need to find someone to kill him. To kill me.

"If someone was able to kill you, they would've by now," Parker points out and I realize I spoke aloud. "You fight every day—and win. The biggest, baddest shifters, the half deranged—anyone who will step into the ring. Sometimes two at a time."

"Ya can't stop fighting," Declan murmurs. "Not that I'm complaining. Business is good. Bets are up. The cops stopped sniffing around, and the Shifter Fight Club in Tucson only made us more famous." He swirls his drink. "The Pit. Home of the King of the Beasts."

Right. And what happens if one day my lion kills someone in the ring?

If I end up like my father, a murderer?

Aw, who am I kidding? I've been a murderer since the first day I shifted in the middle of an engagement in Afghanistan. I thought Smyth could help me control my lion. All he did was make it worse.

I snarl. I'm tempted to walk out, to drive to Denali's house and tell her everything. She might forgive me, once she gets over the shock.

But I can't. Between the flashbacks, the violence, and my lion's insanity, I've built a cage stronger than any Data-X used to hold me.

～

NASH

LATER THAT NIGHT, I head into the ring. The crowd cheers, but all I hear are screams. How many did I kill as a soldier? They're here, ghostlike faces turned vicious, ready to drag me to death.

My vision goes blood red, then black.

Next thing I know, I'm in the ring and Parker signals the

start of the match. The bruin turns, and his profile reminds me of one of the Data-X guards. A sadistic fuck who liked to strap down small shifters and pump them full of juice until they smoked. *Snack-sized,* he said.

Red. Black. The bruin falls, his face a bloody mask. The bouncers enter, drag him out. Another fighter takes his place. Young. Cocky. Like me and the other prisoners when we voluntarily entered testing, thinking we were part of a grand experiment. A master race.

*"We'll find the best for you Nash,"* Dr. Smyth said. *"I'll help you control your lion. Keep him from killing again. And then you'll breed the master race."*

Red. Black. Another fighter in the ring. Two this time. They rush me together and their fists fall. Pain washes me clean.

*I'm back strapped onto the chair, sides bruised. Mouth parched, body smoking. "Not so strong now?" the guard asks, raising the shock stick.*

I roar and two startled faces blur in front of me. I reach through the red haze, grab both by the scruff of their necks and slam their skulls together. Two for one.

The crowd screams. My head rings. Declan stands in front of me, offering water.

"How many fights do I have left?"

"One more." He sounds worried. "But you don't need the fight. We can—"

"No." I climb to my feet as a mean-looking fighter lumbers into the ring. My lion won't be deprived his prey.

"We need to stop it," Declan says to Parker, who nods. "I've never seen him like this."

Parker turns and raises his megaphone. "That's all for tonight, folks—"

The crowd boos. They want blood. I'll give it to them.

I rise to my feet and plod to the center of the ring, the crowd's cries washing over my bruised flesh. "Nash. Nash," they chant. "King of the Beasts."

My opponent turns with a mean smile. I grin back and let loose my lion.

Red. Black. Black. Black.

"Nash, stop, stop!" A grey head flashes in front of me. Parker, shouting, mouth open and wild. "You won. He's down. Stop before you kill him." The air is heavy with the scent of blood. My lion approves.

"You won," Parker repeats. I try to take a step and stagger under the weight of several bouncers. Panic rises, and I thrash to throw them off. No use. The prison guards have shock sticks.

"Let him go," Parker cries and the men release me, jumping back. But I run, claws out. I'm blind, blood streaming into my eyes. I reach the fence. It's not electric. Someone turned the power off. This is my chance.

"Nash—" Declan is on the other side of the fence.

I raise my hands—now tipped with black claws—and swipe through the metal.

My claws tear and I howl but don't stop until there's a hole big enough for a lion to rush through.

Then I run. My lion is out, people are screaming, scrambling out of my way. Red claws at my eyes, black lurking in the corners, threatening. One final burst of speed and I'm outside. Falling to all fours, I let the darkness consume me.

∼

I WAKE naked in the car, my mouth full of blood. I cough on the tang and almost spatter the wrinkled piece of paper lying on the dash. Denali's address. The lion found it and put it there.

"All right. All right."

Every inch of my body screams. My hands are swollen, bloody. Over the past few months, the shifter healing has slowed, and that can only mean one thing: I'm dying. It's only a matter of time. It's only a question of how many I take with me.

I can't risk Denali. But the next time I black out, my lion might take me to her door. There's no telling what he'd do.

He's made it clear, if I let him die, he'll take everyone he can down with him. I have no choice. I have to go to Denali now, when I'm in control.

I find a change of clothes in my trunk and get dressed. I put the car in gear and drive, not sure if I'm a dying man headed for the gallows, or a cure.

# 3

# N*ash*

THE ADDRESS LEADS me to a little house in Temecula. I pull up and idle a moment. My hand shakes as I park. Excitement? Or the last stages of madness?

It's a mistake to come here. I know this as soon as I step onto the little porch, and her scent hits me. Blackness curls from the edges of my vision, pulling me under.

*THE GUARDS HAVE guns on her. My lion surges to the fore, angry. It's been so long since he's killed. But when the naked female stumbles forward, I catch her. My arms close around her body and I pull her soft form against my hard one. She's tall, her head coming just under my chin, soft, dark hair a cloud in my face. The cinnamon scent hits me again, until I taste it.*

*"Another one for you, Nash." The guard's voice is harsh,*

*mocking. They see what I do with the females they bring me. There are cameras in the corners of the room. They watch. I know what they'll do if I refuse: hurt the female. They've learned I don't give a shit what they do to me, but I can't stand to watch someone else be tortured as a result of my choices.*

*For some reason, this one sends an extra blast of protective fury through me. My grip tightens around her. She stiffens.*

*"You know what to do. Get to it. Or else." The threat hangs in the air. I want to tear them apart with my teeth.*

*The door scrapes as they leave.*

*I don't want to move. I could hold her like this for the night, and never feel wanting. But desire's there too, bubbling up, the first hint of warmth after a long winter. With the other females, I had to focus to get myself hard enough to breed them. I spent a long time on foreplay to make sure they were ready and get myself into the right mindset. I'll do that for this one, too, but it won't be for me. My lion's already rumbling for her.*

*She glares up at me like I'm the enemy. I sense anger in her, rising, matching mine. Frustration. A spirit uncowed. Brave. Naked and defenseless, but not afraid.*

*Because I'm angry for her, because I'm furious such a beautiful, fresh lioness would be forced into this awful situation, I snarl.*

*She jerks back, out of my grasp.*

*I immediately reach for her. "I won't hurt you," I promise. My lion needs to soothe her. It's a primordial instinct, like eating or killing. I try to push down the need coiling below my waist.*

*"What are you supposed to do?" she asks. The wariness in her expression tells me she already knows. Her body knows it, too. Her cocoa-tipped nipples stand up, hard and pointed.*

*Filling my lungs with her delicious scent, I tip her face up to mine. "What's your name?"*

. . .

"Denali." I whisper. Inside, my lion waits, patient on this hunt. I follow the cinnamon scent on the air to the screen door.

And I see her. Long, lean limbs, flawless mocha skin. She's barefoot at her kitchen counter, weight on one hip, pert ass encased in cutoff shorts. Her elegant neck curves as she looks down at what she's doing.

Unable to stop myself, I push the door open and enter silently. I'm back in the jungle, a soldier, a predator stalking my prey.

Her head turns slightly.

My lips move to form her name.

Her chocolate brown eyes flare to blue-grey. "Nash?" she chokes.

I walk toward her. She rears back.

"It's all right, Denali." I stop and lift my hands. "I'm not here to hurt you." That's the truth, even if my lion is a crazy mo-fo.

A tremor runs through her. Once, twice, and the spiced scent rises between us.

*Mine,* my lion snarls. *My mate.*

"Denali, I—" my voice cracks but it's too late. She whirls and runs out the back door.

∼

*Denali*

I RUN WITHOUT THINKING. I've been hiding so long; my first instinct is to bolt.

The kitchen door slams behind me. Whenever the weather is nice, I keep the doors and windows open to let in the scent of wildflowers. And to alert me to anyone approaching.

But my lioness was sleeping. Or, perhaps she caught the subtle scent of the soldier she once knew and decided not to tell me. Or I ignored it. Too long I've carried the memory of Nash, the ghost. I see him in my dreams, wake up with the smell of him hanging over me like a cloud. I eat sleep and breathe Nash, even as I run from him.

That's what happens when you're mate marked. You can't escape. You're bonded on the deepest cellular level.

Even after they die.

*I thought he was dead.*

The screen door bangs behind me, and a gust of wind hits my back, spurring me on. Nash is coming after me. The lion is on the hunt.

Glad I'm barefoot, I call on every muscle in my legs, pounding up the hill. I chose this house for its seclusion. Not many people want to live out in the hills, but I found the beauty irresistible. The warm sun, the neat rows of vineyards cutting across the land. Nothing like the grey cell I was trapped in for nine long weeks.

*I should've known he'd come for me.* I saw it on the news. The Data-X lab burned to the ground—the one that held us. Oh, the news didn't call it Data-X. In fact, after the initial report, no news could be found on it at all. Like it got hushed up quickly. But I recognized the location. That wasn't a random wildfire as they later reported. It was a fire set to destroy a prison.

So I waited, breath held. Surely, if Nash was alive, he would come for me. Hadn't he been whispering it every night, in my dreams?

But he didn't come. I figured he was dead, after all. And I'd done nothing to prevent it.

Now he's here. His hot breath reaches the back of my neck and I feint right, then dodge round the scrub brush. The lion follows me easily.

Nash was military. He was one of the strongest, fittest shifters I ever met, and the years did nothing to dull his prowess. I won't get away. I don't even know why I'm running, except that seeing him brought up too much, too fast. He was part of my experience at Data-X. But I know he's not the enemy.

"Denali. Stop."

I put on a burst of speed, dodging around boulders. The one thing my lioness is best at—running.

Only she doesn't want to run. She wants to stay and face the charging lion.

I go too fast and slide on some loose gravel, scraping my hands on the ground as I find my feet again.

"Dammit—you'll hurt yourself."

My chest tightens. Still the gentleman.

*Not as much as you'll hurt me.* My ears ring with my shout. I said it out loud.

"I won't. I promise."

At the pain in his voice, my calves spasm, my feet fumble. My lioness has had enough. She forces me to slow, just enough for the hunter to catch up.

He tackles me and drives me down to the ground, but twists to cushion the fall with his limbs. Oh, this is familiar. Nash on top of me, straddling my body, turning me to face him.

"No, no, no." I whimper. "You're not real. You're not here." If I can't see the monster, he isn't real. Except Nash isn't the monster.

He pulls my hands down roughly. I'm pinned, his body on mine. Mine responding with alacrity. My lioness in awe.

*Foolish, wanton animal.* I can't just throw caution to the wind. To give myself up to a male I barely know.

"Denali," he rasps. Face to face, I see he hasn't changed. Maybe a little leaner, a little harder, but same smooth cheeks, military cut hair, scar in his eyebrow. He's so beautiful he makes my chest hurt. Of course, he's also on top of me—but that feels right. My hips lift without my permission.

"It's you. It's really you." His eyes blaze gold. The lion came out with the chase. I make myself go limp under him. I can't best him in a one-on-one fight. If he does mean me harm, my only hope is to get him to let his guard down, and escape.

*He doesn't mean you harm,* my lioness whispers. But I see a wildness in his eyes and my body tenses with uncertainty.

He brushes my face with the backs of his fingers and I let out a whimper. I can't do this. It's too painful, too raw.

"Why do you think I'll hurt you?"

I shake my head as if to jostle my thoughts into place. Get my twisted emotions out of it. Running was just a PTSD related reaction. After what I survived, who wouldn't have post-traumatic stress? It wasn't fueled by thought. I took one look at the male who's haunted my dreams and bolted.

"I'm not going to hurt you."

"You already did," I sob before I can bite my lips. I don't even know this male. We spent one night together in a prison cell, forced to mate under duress. He marked me. End of story. I don't know why I'm acting like he's a lover who abandoned me. Like I gave him my heart to begin with. I wouldn't be so naive.

And yet not a day's gone by since then I haven't ached for him. Wondered what my life would be like if he were by my side, as a true mate should be. In the years since,

I've thought about finding a real mate—one I chose voluntarily. But I couldn't even bring myself to go on a single date. No male compared to this magnificent one, this king of beasts.

"Denali." He cups my cheek with his warm, rough hand and my lioness leans into his touch. "Please," he whispers, and brushes his lips over mine. My back arches automatically and I push into the kiss. He tastes like spice, surrender. Like home.

He drops his head into the crook of my neck and inhales deeply. His body reacts to my scent, erection punching out and pressing between my legs, a low growl sounding from his throat.

I'm pinned under a large, randy male but there's not an ounce of fight in me. Instead—fates help me—I rock my damp sex over the bulge in his jeans. He stamps his lips over mine, claiming my mouth as he draws up my t-shirt and cups my breast. I writhe under him, desperate for more contact. The air grows heavy with a cinnamon scent. One sniff of Nash and my lioness is in heat.

But this is crazy. We're not lovers. We're not even friends. We are two shifters who were forced together under horrifying circumstances. We can't just pick up where we left off, because that's not a place I ever want to return to.

"No." I break off the kiss, gasping.

"Can't stop," he murmurs urgently, still moving his lips over mine. He nips at the corner of my mouth. "You taste so good."

Damn, he tastes good, too. And having him devour my mouth like a starving man does something powerful to my libido. It's like my sexuality has been in a coma since we've been apart and now, under his touch, it revs back to life. He has an arm under me, cushioning me even as he holds me fast. I'm a tall, strong woman, but under Nash I feel small. Delicate.

Beautiful.

His hand moves down from my breast over my flat midriff, sliding straight into my shorts.

I suck in a breath, desire igniting in my core.

His eyes flare with amber light. "Mine," he growls.

"No." I don't mean *no* I don't want him in my shorts. But no, my pussy isn't *his*. He may have marked me, but that mark doesn't count.

I don't belong to him.

The only shifter I belong to is Nolan.

I fight for sanity, even as he palms my mons and strokes along my juicy opening. "This is—"

He stops my protest with another savage kiss, his mouth dominating, claiming. Shivers run up my spine. I dig my heels into the ground and push into his hand working between my legs.

He presses a finger into me, rubs the heel of his hand against my clit.

My orgasm blows up like a summer storm—beautiful, wild. Devastating.

I close my throat to keep from moaning his name as he makes my body dance. Just like the last time we were together, our connection is magnetic. I want to refuse, but my body, my lioness, has other ideas.

I cling to him, panting. This, like our entire relationship, is fucked up. And yet it feels so right.

"Beautiful lioness."

I sag in his embrace, mind swirling with worry even as my body soars with the stars.

We only shared one night, in a cell with guards watching the cameras outside, but it changed the course of our lives. I knew that as much as he did. As much as I told myself to forget Nash, to forget that night, I couldn't stop. I longed for him like no other. My body remembered his touch. I couldn't forget his strength, his tortured soul, his gentleness. Our incredible chemistry. We only had one night in a prison, but we created something real.

The truth is scary. I ran from it as much as I did to escape Data-X, and the lion who marked me as mate.

Nash's eyes still glow yellow, and he watches me with a predatory stare. One that promises retribution. For leaving him. For running. For denying his claim. His lion won't let me go—not without a fight.

He eases his fingers from me and brings the digits to his mouth, tasting them. All the while, watching me.

I don't even know where to begin with this male, so I go for the inane. "You keep your hair so short." His hair, so short and bristly, is softer than it looks. I run my palm over it and a rush of emotion steals my breath. I don't want to stop touching him.

"Force of habit," he mutters.

"You should grow it out. I want to see what it looks like long. Shaggy lion."

The corners of his mouth ease. The rest of him is tense. I should be the one who's tense, but I'm not. At least my body isn't. I just had an incredible orgasm.

Now that my focus has returned, I scan his face, noting new hollows under his cheekbones, a half-healed cut near his temple beside a fading bruise. Why hasn't he regenerated?

I shift beneath his heavy frame and the animal in him recedes, the gentleman I remember returning. He pulls away from me, like he just realized the position we're in.

"I'm sorry," he mutters and scrambles to his feet, helping me to stand. "I didn't mean to... ah..."

"Assert your claim?" I finish wryly, brushing the dust off my ass. "Oh, I imagine you did."

I don't expect the misery that swims over his expression. It washes over me, his emotions bleeding over mine and I have to fight to push the darkness back. Whatever happened to Nash after that night, it left him maimed.

It drives a spike of fear through me, even as my heart squeezes.

*Fix him*, my lioness whispers.

But I can't.

Just like I couldn't go back. There's more than one life that hangs in the mix, and that life is more important than mine or his. At least to me, it is.

Around us the birds continue singing their celebration, oblivious to the two predators who invade their territory. My house looks lonely far below past a slope of wildflowers dancing in the wind.

I fix my gaze on it to keep from looking at Nash. "How'd you find me?"

"Started searching as soon as I got out. My friends helped."

I stiffen. How long has he been out? How much did his friends uncover?

"Don't worry," he soothes. "They'll keep your location secret. They only told me."

This doesn't reassure me. I can't afford for Nash to be a part of my life. There's too much at stake.

Of course, my rash lioness is just fine with Nash turning up. She's purring. I take a moment to sense his animal and a queasiness returns.

"Your lion is upset."

"My lion is a sick fuck."

I force myself to look at him, to search his haunted eyes. "They hurt you."

"Yes. But I was fucked up before I went to them."

"Why'd you come, Nash?"

Pain flickers over his face, dark with a storm I can't decipher. "How could I not? I marked you. You belong to me." He fists a hand in my curls and tugs my head to the side to find the place where his teeth scored my skin. When he lowers his mouth and traces the barely visible mark with his tongue, I shiver. My pussy clenches as if affirming his ownership over me.

"Why'd you run from me, Denali?"

I hear hurt in his voice—or is it warning? Will there be punishment? Shockingly, the thought excites me. I push the image of him tying me to the bed and asserting his ownership over my body again and again from my mind. "Are you afraid of me? Can you tell I—" he breaks off, eyes shuttering.

"I thought you were dead."

"You thought you were seeing a ghost?"

I shake my head. He continues to trail the tip of his tongue over my skin, tracing the column of my neck, flicking my earlobe. Memories of what he can do with his tongue between my legs crowd the rational thoughts from my mind.

His body presses against mine, long and muscular and oh so right.

"I should have died. I feel half-dead most of the time since I got out."

"But... you cooperated." I swallowed. "I heard you volunteered to the program."

I'll never forget the day the men in suits showed up at my grandfather's place. First they were slick-talkers. Trying to tell me I'd been chosen for a special study. My grandfather and aunt stood in front of me. Said no way they were taking me.

They drew guns, asked me to come or they'd kill my family. My grandfather and aunt screamed for me to shift and run. They weren't going to give me up.

And now they're dead.

Rage mixes with pain in Nash's expression. His nostrils flare, jaw flexes. "I did cooperate. Hell, I volunteered for the damn study. Until I figured out what they were doing."

"Master race," I mutter and his eyes blaze lion bright. His grip in my hair tightens.

When I wince, he immediately releases me, stepping back. "You escaped not long after I claimed you."

There it is. But I don't hear any accusation in his tone.

Still, guilt swims over me. "I saw my chance and took it."

"Good. I'm glad. It made things... easier, knowing you got out of that hellhole." The wind picks up. I shiver, and he shifts to block me from the chill. I don't think he does it consciously, but his care warms me from head to toe.

# 4

## Nash

DENALI'S GONE pale and my lion's snarling, wanting to fix whatever's broken here. Except how does a ruined lion fix anything?

"I'm sorry—I wasn't in any position to go back for you." Her fingers bunch and twist.

My brows shoot up. Jesus. Is that what she's upset about? She's suffered survivor guilt all this time?

Fuck, I know more than a little bit about that. My flashbacks aren't only from Data-X. They're from Afghanistan, too.

I can't stop myself from snatching her shoulders and pulling her into me until we're nose to nose. "You think I would've wanted that?" I don't mean to sound so harsh, but I need her to understand this. Need to help her release the guilt. "*Never.* I never wanted you near that place. You getting free was the only goddamn comfort I had in there. Understand?"

She blinks up at me, her chocolate brown eyes glinting with gold and caramel in the light. She's pierced her nose since I saw her last. A tiny gold hoop loops through one nostril. It's fucking perfect on her. Her hair is back to its natural brown, too. When I met her, she'd bleached the tight curls a tawny gold.

Her throat moves as she swallows. "I'm sorry."

I force myself to release her. "No, I'm glad you got out. And I understand why you stayed in hiding."

For a brief moment she stiffens, and my lion knows something's off again, but I have no idea what. She changes the subject. "I heard the lab burned down. Did you...?"

"Yeah. That's when I got out." I confirm. "And I helped burn the second lab, too. Bombed both places to the ground. Dr. Smyth is dead."

"Good," she says fiercely. Our gazes meet and for once, we're on the same page. Both of us burning for revenge.

She clears her throat and looks down at her neatly trimmed fingernails. "I ran out of habit. Years of looking over my shoulder. Afraid someone would hunt me down and drag me back to that place. I guess... I saw you and panicked."

*Thank fuck.*

I'm breathing faster than normal at her confession.

She's not afraid of me. Her instincts took over as she ran. Except shouldn't her instincts tell her I'm safe? That I'm the one guy who would never, ever hurt her? The one who would die to protect her?

Or are her instincts as damaged as mine?

My gut twists as a new thought hits me. *She ran because I am a danger to her.* I shouldn't have come—I'm a fucking loose cannon. But I keep clinging to the hope that being with her will heal my sick lion.

I have nothing to offer but a damaged soul and a dying body. But worse, the violence in me eats me from the inside out. And I would never, ever put her in danger. I'm not my father.

"And now?"

She licks her lips and I track the movement of her tongue. My balls draw up tighter. "It's ah... good to see you. I'm glad you made it out, too."

It isn't an invitation. Not really, but I can't stop my hands from sliding onto her hips, then around to her firm backside. She's built like an athlete—with long, lean runner's legs and the perfect amount of junk in the trunk.

She stumbles up against me when I pull her closer. Not resisting, but not giving in yet, either. Of course, she has no reason to surrender to me. Her lioness may know its mate, but the two of us? We're practically strangers.

She doesn't feel like a stranger to me, though.

"You gonna invite me in? Just for cup of coffee or something?" My lion's ready to throw her over my shoulder and carry her straight to her bedroom, but the more civil part of me remembers to rein it in. Take it slow. She bolted out the door the minute she saw me, for fates' sake. She's not going to lie back and offer herself up on a platter.

She hesitates. "Yeah. Sure. But I have somewhere to be by 4 p.m."

I settle my hand on her lower back and guide her back to her place. As we reach her back gate, I stoop to pick a little purple blossom and offer it to her. "Favorite flower."

Some of her wariness eases, a smile tugging at the corners of her mouth. "Wildflower." She takes it and brings it to her nose. "I can't believe you remembered."

"I remember everything about that night." That's the truth. Sometimes I can't remember my own name, but I will never, ever forget the moments I had with Denali. My lioness.

～

*Denali*

*The door closes with a final clang. They delivered me, naked, to this male. I don't know how long I've been captive—a week or so—but it's long enough to know the guards are trouble. They treat me all right, but other prisoners aren't so lucky.*

*A low growl rumbles in the male's throat, but it's not for me. His arms banded around me protectively the moment they pulled the sheet away and tossed me in. He's big, solid. His hair is military short, and his stance reminds me of a soldier. But he's not a human. He's a lion, like me.*

*"So." I blow out a breath. "What do we do now?"*

*He holds me, his body angled in a way I realize hides me from the cameras. I'm tall, with a strong, athletic build, but he's even bigger. I hunch against him, grateful for the protection.*

*"They shouldn't bother us the rest of the night, if we cooperate," he says. "I'm Nash. What's your name?"*

*"Denali Decker."*

*"Pleased to meet you," he says.*

*I take a step away from him. Is he serious? This isn't a fucking date. As soon as I pull away his hands drop. I sense him being careful not to move, scare me, and it makes me even more angry. "What does it mean to cooperate?"*

*He glances to the bed, and away. I've been in this place long enough to know what he means.*

*I shake my head. "This is fucked up." I whirl on my toes to face the door, ready to rant, ready to pound the walls and demand to be let out, to be treated with common decency.*

*"Don't." There's urgency in his tone. I turn. His shoulders are tense, and his eyes blaze—not with anger or defiance. No, it's worry. Warning. He's afraid for me. "Please, don't."*

*Fates. To see such a big strong warrior afraid sends spikes of fear through me. What chance do I have in here? "You're not going to fight?"*

*He shakes his head. "Not with you here."*

*"You're strong enough to take them."*

*"Some of them. But not all. And then they'll hurt you."*

*Just like that my bravado is gone. Who am I kidding? They killed my pride right in front of my eyes. Shot them with quick, military precision. My beloved grandfather with a bullet through the skull. I'd do anything to go back and cooperate. If I had, I might have saved them.*

*I wrap my arms around myself. "So we're just supposed to..." I nod to the bed. "And if I don't..."*

*Again, he shields me from the camera, herds me back toward the cot without touching me. "We'll do what they tell us to do," he says, but I think it's more for the watchers. I sense he's trying to convey something else to me. His gaze is intent, bursting with a message. Or a promise. He's not going to hurt me.*

*The backs of my knees hit the cot and I sit down. He crouches in front of me, hands on my thighs. The silent communication is still there. Like he's willing me to understand something.*

*Every cell in my body is suddenly aware of the nearness of his masculine form. Even though I'm appalled by our situation, a slow thrum begins to pulse between my legs. I imagine those strong hands sliding higher.*

*"Shouldn't you buy me dinner first?" I try to joke.*

*His thumbs stroke tiny circles on the insides of my legs.*

*Something flutters in my belly. Excitement? Can't be.*

"This is so fucked up," I repeat. "We don't even know each other."

"Gold," he says.

"What?"

"My favorite color is gold. What's yours?"

"I... purple." *If he wants to play this inane game while the guards watch via camera, who am I to argue?*

"Purple and gold," he muses. "The colors of royalty."

"The lion is the king of the beasts," *I point out dryly, and, sure enough, his mouth twists in a grimacing smile at the irony. Two powerful apex predators, locked in a cell together. Forced to breed.*

*My breath catches. My gaze falls to his hands, large and rawboned. Powerful enough to kill, but his touch is gentle. Maybe tonight won't be so bad. Fates, what if it was actually... good?*

*When I meet his gaze, he's watching me. My cheeks heat.*

"Favorite flower?" *he asks.*

"I don't have one. I like whatever's in season—growing in the wild."

"Wildflowers." *He tilts his head, a half-smile spreading over his handsome face. It makes him look younger, almost boyish.* "See?" *He squeezes my leg playfully.* "We're getting to know each other."

I BLINK AT THE FLOWER, willing myself not to tremble. Nash and I shared only one night, but it seemed to encompass an eternity.

He tucks the flower behind my ear, and I gasp at the state of his knuckles, the swollen, bruised skin. Why hasn't he regenerated? Something's wrong with his lion.

"What happened to your hands?"

"Fights."

Panic steals my breath. "Data-X?"

Violence surges into the air just at the mention of the sadistic, government-backed company that imprisoned us. The one that promised me control of my lion but ended up being nothing but gene mining, forced breeding, and endurance testing/torture.

"Not them. I fight for a living. I have to. My lion—he needs to fight."

I take a moment to sense his animal again. There's a wild, reckless quality to it, almost like static, never settling. "He's sick."

"Definitely." Nash slides his arms around me suddenly, and I go still as he presses his face to my neck. "I tried to stay away. But I need you." His voice drops an octave, guttural sound. "*Mate.*"

My breath hitches. I have nothing to offer this male. I'm barely scraping by myself. And yet it's literally impossible for me to push him away.

He needs me. He's broken, and I might be able to heal him. "Shhhh." I stroke his back. "It's all right. I'm here." *For now.*

"Denali, I can't..." He raises his head and I kiss him. I can't give him much, but I can give this moment. This connection. Bodies seeking pleasure together. Animals communing.

I can give him what he gave me last time. Make it good. I *want* to do this for him.

Oh, who am I kidding? I want this for me, too.

Instantly, his hands grip my ass, and he lifts me easily. I wrap my legs around his waist, dragging my needy core over the bulge of his cock.

"Bedroom?" he pauses enough to ask.

"Second door on the left." I weave my arms around his

neck, kissing him hard. I have a moment of panic when he almost stumbles into the wrong room, but he kicks open the correct door and lays me on the bed.

"Is this okay?" He frowns. He knows I'm hiding something. Or he's still the gentleman.

I sit up and pull off my t-shirt. His hungry gaze lands on the swell of my breasts above my red bra. "I need you." It's the truth. I pull him down on top of me, craving his delicious weight between my legs. The scent of vanilla and cinnamon rises between us. I kiss him hard, tongue darting between his lips. I'm desperate for him to be with me, to believe me, and not dig up secrets better left unsaid.

There's a frown between his brows, but it doesn't stop him from taking charge like I knew he would. He moves on top of me, settling his hips in the cradle of my legs as his tongue thrusts into my mouth.

"Denali," he breathes, his hand rough on my breast. He yanks down the cups of my bra and feasts on one nipple, nipping and sucking and pinching it before he moves to the other one.

I moan, legs thrashing beneath him, pelvis thrusting up to rub my needy parts over his erection.

I pull his t-shirt up, rake my nails over his skin. He growls, hips snapping.

"Do you have a condom?" I gasp.

He jerks back, blinking as the amber glow of his eyes fades to hazel. "Yeah." His voice is two octaves deeper than usual. He digs out his wallet and produces a condom.

I reach for the button on his jeans, but he grabs my wrists and pins them beside my head. "I need to taste you first," he growls.

*Oh fates, yes.*

"You gonna be a good girl and keep your hands up here while I lick you, baby? Or do I need to tie you up?"

Holy hell, it's like he tapped right into the fantasy I had earlier.

I push my wrists against him. "I'm never a good girl."

It's a challenge, and I'm not sure whether he'll take it. We don't know each other well enough for sex games, really. Hell, I don't even know enough about sex with other shifters to know if this kind of play is safe.

Except it feels so right. And Nash's answering grin is pure wickedness. Keeping my hands pinned with one of his large palms, he rolls me over and works open the clasp on my bra.

"Do you know what happens to bad girls, Denali?" He ties my hands with the bra in seconds flat. A true boy scout. Or soldier.

"What?"

He rolls my hips to the side and slaps my ass. It's a hard, commanding slap and it goes straight to my core. My pussy clenches and a shaky mewl slips out of my mouth.

His grin widens. "Oh baby, I've imagined claiming you again for a thousand nights, but I never pictured it this way."

I lick my lips. My ass tingles where he smacked me and the pulse in my clit takes all my attention. "Why not?"

He lets out a harsh curse and smacks me again, twice, then returns me to my back and works open the button on my shorts. "Need this pussy," he growls. "Gotta taste."

I'm unbelievably wet by the time he gets my shorts down. He's still dressed, and I'm fully bared to him, which only makes me hotter. I slide my legs wide as he kisses down my shuddering belly. He flicks my belly button with his tongue, then licks his way lower. Hooking his hands under my knees, he spreads me wide.

"Is all this for me, baby?" he asks before tracing my inner lips with his tongue.

I jerk against him, but he holds my pelvis down, getting on with business.

And he definitely means business.

I haven't forgotten Nash's skill in bed, but after such a long drought, it's even more devastating. Every flick of his tongue has me moaning. My wrists are bound together with the bra, but it's not attached to anything so I bring my hands down to grip his head. He doesn't have enough hair to pull, but I push him down, lift my pelvis to rub up.

He toys with my outer lips, nipping me.

I moan and writhe, needing more.

He sucks my clit, then works two fingers inside me.

I start coming almost immediately, he finger-fucks me roughly, pounding his knuckles to get deeper while his tongue flicks rapidly over my most sensitive nerve-bundle.

"Nash!"

"Aw, that's it, baby. Come for me. I need to see you come."

"Yes, *yes!*" I scream, my pussy squeezing and releasing as the storm passes through me.

He slows the movements of his fingers until it becomes a slow undulation, then a possessive cupping of my mons. He rises over me and kisses me hard, my scent on his lips.

He works the bra off my wrists while he kisses me, but then surprises me by flipping me to my belly and binding my wrists behind my back.

Oh goodie.

I've never had sex like this. Never playful. Never kinky. Nash was already the epitome of masculine attractiveness to me, but this? This is like sex in another dimension. It's every fantasy and desire I've had plus all those I never dared dream rolled up into one.

"Since you're having a hard time with your hands, I'll have to give you a little more help." Nash's breath is short, like he's already panting for release.

He's already brought me to orgasm twice—he must have balls the color of blueberries.

"And I think you liked having your ass smacked, didn't you, baby?"

I tense for more spanking, but it doesn't come. I realize he's waiting for my reply.

"Yes," I admit.

"*Yes, sir,* is usually how this works." There's a chuckle in his voice.

I'm getting swoony just over the fact that he *knows* how this works. Whatever *this* is.

"Yes, sir." My voice is so husky I don't recognize it.

He lifts my hips until my knees slide up under me, so I'm resting on my upper body with my ass in the air. "Mmm, now that's a beautiful sight." He slaps my ass a couple times. I want more, but he reaches for the condom. I hear the crinkle of the packet and then he's there, pressing at my entrance.

"*Yes.*" I utter the word like his cock is my salvation. Maybe it is. I want him so badly. Want the sensation of him filling me. Claiming me. Using me.

He groans as he pushes in, his large cock angled perfectly to seat deeply. His hands grip my hips, fingers digging in. He doesn't move. I feel his thighs shake against mine, the pulse of his thick manhood inside me.

"Fuck, Denali. Fuck. You feel so good. Better than I remembered. Better than anything." He's babbling. Offering his words up to the Gods of Sex. Of lions and lionesses.

Finally, he moves. Out and then *in*. He slams home like he couldn't stand the half second of retreat. "Baby, I'm losing my mind already."

Who am I to complain? He already got me off twice. But I start giving orders. "Fuck me, Nash. I need it harder."

He curses and jackhammers into me, stuffing me so full of his cock I lose my mind, too. *Slap-slap-slap.* His loins smack against my ass, his balls catch my clit. He drives deeper and harder and faster.

My eyes roll back in my head, my teeth chatter.

His roar bounces off the walls. I scream. We both come in a monumental orgasm.

Before I can recover, he's freed my hands from the bra and he pushes me to my belly. His fingers lace over the top of mine as he fucks me slowly, taking his time now, like he's savoring the feel of me. Or he doesn't want it to end.

Hell, I don't either.

My mind is beyond blown. I'm still orbiting the moon.

Nash's mouth finds my neck. He bites and kisses and sucks. Traces the place where he marked me.

My pussy squeezes his cock. My lioness purrs.

Nash releases one of my hands and works his under my hips. Still rocking in and out of me, he lazily rubs my clit. I'm not ready to orgasm again. I'm too relaxed. Too replete.

Nash isn't in a hurry. It's just pleasure for the sake of pleasure now. No rushing to a finish line. Just two bodies communing. Two animals purring.

My mind wants to race around this problem. Figure out what to do with Nash when we're done. How to side-step our connection. But my lioness won't let my mind follow any thread of thought. It's only the rightness of Nash moving inside me, the glory of his touch, his scent.

And just when I reach the point where I need Nash to

either stop or move forward, he pounces—quick, and powerful. I find myself on my back, Nash shoving my knees wider to make way for his thighs. "Gotta fuck you again, my queen." He thrusts into me.

I gasp at the power of the drive. My mouth opens with a cry, head falling back, chin arched to the ceiling.

And then he's driving hard again. The king of beasts, plowing his way home.

Lights explode behind my eyes. I'm suspended in time—hurled into an explosion of carnal pleasure. I think the snarling sound comes from me, but I can't be sure. The room shakes with our roars, bed slamming against the wall.

He fucks me way too hard, but I love every second of it. I crave this pounding contact, need more, more, more.

"Yes, Nash—*yes*!" I scream. My nails dig into his back, I think I bite him, although I'm not sure where. My eyes flip back in my head and the room spins.

"Nash, oh fates, Nash," I mumble, chanting his name on repeat mode until the swells smooth and I'm floating on a still, quiet bed of blankets.

Nash crashes beside me, his chest heaving, sweat glistening on his light brown chest hair curls. I trace the tattoos across his chest. He turns into me and strokes a hand up my side to cup a breast. "Keep saying my name like that, my queen, and I'll never let you out of this bed."

∼

NASH

. . .

My world—no, my entire universe—just shifted and rearranged. This is where I belong. In Denali's bed. Satisfying my mate.

Except I have nothing to offer her but a ruined animal and a male who fights with his fists for his dinner.

Still, my beast kneads his paws, a new strength pouring through my veins. Just being with Denali, mating with her again, revives my tattered spirit. I don't know why I need my mate so much, but I do. It's the first time I've lifted my head and looked around since I broke out of the lab. No, since before Afghanistan.

Denali doesn't look at me, caught in her own musings.

Fates—I have no clue what she thinks of all this. Our physical attraction is undeniable, yes. But while she appears content, she's not giving off the *let's move in together and play house* energy. No, she's definitely giving off a solitary lioness vibe. More like, *thanks for the orgasms, catch ya on the flip side.*

I should give her space.

*No space,* my lion growls. *Don't let her out of your sight again.*

But that's crazy. I'm not a stalker. Okay, yeah, I just chased her up a hill and tackled her to the ground, but I couldn't help myself.

And that's precisely why I need to give her space. My lion is not well. I'm dangerous. And I definitely don't want to fuck this up.

I sit up and roll off the bed, recalling that she had to leave by 4 p.m.

∽

*Denali*

. . .

"What time is it?" I reach for my phone and get a chill. It's almost 4 p.m. "I have to go." I rise and grab my shorts.

"I know." Nash bends over to tie his boots, gorgeous muscles glowing in the lazy afternoon light. There's a heaviness to his tone that makes my chest tight.

He knows what I'm going to say.

So I say it. "Yeah. You should go." I face the wall as I shrug on a shirt, wincing at how cold I sound. "I'm sorry. I have a life. A job."

I barely hear a step before he's at my back. "This isn't over, Denali."

My heart lurches and skids. Of course not. It's too much to ask, to share one more afternoon and then part ways.

"I'm late. I have to go. Please, Nash." I turn to plead with him.

His expression is shuttered. He nods.

"It's probably not a good idea for you to come back."

Well, that came out sounding wishy-washy. Because my lioness is scrambling my brain. She doesn't want him to walk away. I'm not even sure I want him to walk away. But I definitely need to proceed with caution. It's not just about me. I have Nolan to protect.

His frown tells me he doesn't agree.

"Walk me to the door?"

He escorts me with a hand on my back. Ever the gentleman. He had manners, even when we were trapped in a cell.

"So where do you live? How can I get in touch?"

"I'm in San Diego. Not far. I'll give you my number."

I enter his phone number into my cell. He doesn't ask for mine in return, but if he found me here, he probably already has it. "It was good to see you." I mean it. As troubled as I am by his appearance, I also hate saying goodbye. I lock the door. "I've got to run." I kiss him on the cheek—and jog to my car. Somehow he arrives before me, and opens the door.

I get in and focus on turning on the car, ignoring him as he leans over me. "I'm sorry," I repeat. "But I'm late. I really have to go."

I pull out of the drive, leaving him standing there, watching me go. Everything in me wants to turn back, run into his arms, tell him everything.

I shake my head, and the flower falls out of my hair. Somehow in all our lovemaking, it hung on. Until now. It lies on the floor, battered but still beautiful. Like the lion I left. A brutal fighter with a sick animal. My mate.

What the hell am I going to do?

～

*Nash*

I FOLLOW Denali's beat up hatchback through town. She's hiding something. Normally I wouldn't stalk a female, but my lion insists. She's my mate. Even if I'm in no shape to take care of her.

She's done well for herself. From the information Sam forwarded, she has her own small business running errands and taking care of homebound elderly. She pays most everything in cash. Still living mostly under the radar.

Her old car runs a yellow light and I pull through a gas station parking lot to keep her in my sights. She wasn't kidding about being late. Either that she drives like a maniac. No matter. I catch up with her easily, almost pulling flush with her car. She doesn't notice me following her. A little frown of concentration mars her forehead.

## Alpha's War    43

My lion admires her. He hasn't been this happy in... ever. My animal was born in blood, triggered in battle. I've never known him to be anything but a stone-cold killer.

Except with Denali. Drumming my hands on the steering wheel, I realize I'm grinning.

She let me into her bed, even though she wasn't entirely happy to see me. But afterward, she certainly was in a hurry to get me out of her life. That just shows she's smart. No matter. Even if I should, I'm not about to let her go.

She stops briefly at a grocery store, coming out with two bags before continuing on. She must have more errands because she doesn't head home, but back to the main boulevard until she turns into the parking lot of a low building with a fenced playground.

What is she doing at a preschool?

Denali disappears into the building. A minute later, she exits, holding the hand of a little boy.

My entire body turns to ice.

*A cub.*

She has a cub. But... who's the father? She wasn't pregnant when she met me, and I mate-marked her. Who would dare touch her after that? A human? As I blink away the red haze, there's a crunching sound. I broke the steering wheel. I tear open the car door, my legs eating up sidewalk. *Mine,* my lion growls. *Mine.*

Denali looks up. Shock and fear cross her face, followed by anger. The little boy has his head down, oblivious. She steps in front of him.

"*Stay back*, Nash." Her chest rises and falls. She's gearing up to fight me. Momma lioness prepared to protect her cub.

Does she think I'll hurt him?

Well yeah, I did storm out of the car mad as fuck. She's right to fear me. Hell, even I fear my lion most days.

The spice of her scent hits me and I stop in my tracks. The little boy peers around her. I suck in a breath.

His face and hair are pure Denali, only a few shades lighter. But the boy's eyes are green, like mine.

∼

*Denali*

*No, no, no.*

"Nash," I warn. "Back off."

He does, stepping off the sidewalk. I hurry Nolan past him and get my son into his car seat.

"Here, baby." I hand him a juice box and his usual snack. *Just keep calm. Stay normal.* Even though all my plans have gone to hell.

"Who's that, momma?"

I glance back. Nash is rooted, staring right at Nolan. His son.

"He's a... friend."

The boy sniffs, scents the air. "He's like me. He's a lion."

"Yeah, baby. But we don't talk about our animals in public, remember?" I shut the car door, and head to face Nash.

Damn, this is so fucked up.

"What the hell?" Nash chokes out.

"Quiet," I hiss, even though he's only said what I'm thinking.

"Who is that?"

"My kid." I lift my chin and hold my ground.

"How old is he?"

I close my eyes, willing this moment away. I've imagined

it a hundred, a thousand times. I don't know whether I wanted it to happen, or just knew it would.

"Denali, how old?"

"Three," I whisper. "He's three." I'm almost dizzy, helpless to stop this moment. For the past three years, my whole life has been centered around protecting this one vulnerability: my sweet boy, currently eating his goldfish and drinking his juice in his car seat.

"He's mine." He starts to push past me, but I block his path.

"Stay back," I warn.

He stops, craning his head to look around me. "You don't want me near him." It's a statement, not a question and it hits me like a two by four across the ribs.

He's right, I don't.

And yet, haven't I wished a thousand times that Nolan had his daddy in his life? Haven't I imagined what a good father Nash would be?

But that was a different Nash. One I conjured out of memories and fantasy. One who doesn't exist. This Nash looks like he's barely holding on to basic living.

My shoulders sag. "Nash, I just—I don't want him hurt. I can't let him get attached to someone who's not going to be a part of his life."

A muscle in Nash's jaw flexes. "Who says I'm not sticking around?"

I press my lips together. "I never said you could."

It's the wrong thing to say. He has a legal right to be in his son's life whether I want it or not, but he doesn't challenge me. He rubs his stubbled jaw, still trying to peer past me at our son.

The static-y quality to his animal grows louder.

I shiver, my lioness senses telling me I've made a mistake, but I ignore them.

"You have a son." The awe in his tone would make more sense if he'd said *we have a son.* The omission sets off alarm bells for me.

"Yeah. His name is Nolan. He's pretty awesome." I ignore the stabbing desire to share Nolan with Nash—for him to review and soak in every milestone he's missed. To laugh with me over the cuteness I endure on a daily basis. To love him as much as I do.

"Denali," Nash chokes. "I didn't know."

I can't stop myself, the words tumble out and expand between us. "Come back this weekend. Maybe we could go to a park and hang out or something. You can meet him. *If you don't tell him you're his dad.*"

~

*Agent Dune*

Charlie scales the rope hanging from the skylight of his target's mansion and slips out, gently replacing and sealing the domed covering.

Bugs successfully planted in international smuggler Duke Ducey's home. He had to rush back from his personal jaunt to Tucson to obey these orders.

Quiet as a cat, he slips over the edge of the roof, hangs from his hands, and throws his body away from the house, over the seven-foot metal fence. Landing noiselessly in a deep squat, he pulls up the black mask that covered his pale skin and stays in the shadows as he walks swiftly up the block to where he parked a car under cover of some bushes.

He calls his handler as he drives away. "It's done. Feed should be live. Check it."

"Already on it," Agent Ann Gray sings, the clack of her fingers flying over keys audible in the background. She's a thirty-something analyst—never been in the field, but highly utilized for information security and transmission. "Yep, feed is live. I'll have it stored on the Degas server and to yours. Anything you want me to monitor for?"

"No, I'll handle it." He hesitates. "I need you to look for something else for me, though. For a different case."

"You bet. What it is?"

"A lab in Mexico City that burned to the ground eighteen months ago."

She goes quiet. "This is a personal request?" There's a tautness in her voice.

*Fuck.* He doesn't know Gray well enough to ask this favor. She seems eager to please, but that means she's eager to please her superiors, too. *Their* superiors.

The ones who told him to stop nosing around the Data-X case. His job had been to bury it. Not dig it up.

*You don't know what you are.* The taunt of Jared Johnson, the cage fighter he picked up and questioned in Tucson rings in his ears.

He'd trailed Nash's associates—the ones connected with the lab fire—to Arizona, where they staged another fight. Charlie got inside, but the local police showed up and blew his cover. His only option was to take over—to make sure they pulled in Jared, one of the fighters, for questioning. Because Charlie saw his eyes change, just like Nash's had in Afghanistan. Just like he remembered his father's changing. Jared is one of them—the superhumans who'd been created or enhanced in the government-funded Data-X lab. And Charlie needed to know more about the project. How his father was connected. What happened to him.

And his government clearance didn't go high enough to get that information. He was chasing it down on his own. And after Jared's comment, the pursuit became something beyond curiosity. Now it borders on obsession.

He researched everyone around Jared—from his pretty blonde attorney to her partner Garrett Green, whose name is behind the warehouses where the illegal fights were being held in Tucson, to Garrett's sister, Sedona, who had a missing person report filed on her in Mexico. All of the people associated with the fights were in Mexico City at the time of the lab fire, just like the San Diego cage fighters had been involved in the Data-X fire.

Yet he hadn't found much in the government files on the Mexico City lab. Not even redacted, above his pay grade information.

"Yeah, it's personal." He blew it his breath and waited.

Gray waits a beat. "Am I going to get in trouble for looking?"

He recognizes his opportunity. She hasn't refused yet. She wants to help. "I haven't been given a direct order not to investigate."

She lets out a strangled laugh. "That's probably because no one knows what you're up to."

Does she? She must know something about Mexico to even question his motives here.

"Tell me something, Dune. Why are you so interested in these lab fires? Did you lose someone?"

He hesitates. "Yeah." It's a lie, but he hopes it will gain her sympathy. Could be a huge mistake, though. If she thinks he's out for revenge, she might not give him anything.

"I'm sorry." Her voice is soft. "I'll look into the lab. I don't think we had anything to do with that one, though."

"That's what I'd gathered, too. Anything you can get would help—what they're studying, who they experimented on. Thanks, Gray."

"Someday I might need a favor."

The corners of his lips turn up. Favors for favors. What could the lovely play-it-safe Ann Gray need from him?

Intriguing.

"Then you'll know where to come." He disconnects the call and stows his phone.

Soon. He might have answers after a lifetime of wondering who—no, what—his father was.

# 5

# N*ash*

I SIT ON A PARK BENCH, watching the little boy named Nolan play in the sandbox. He's bright-eyed and alert, filling a bucket and using a shovel to pat the sand down. Smart kid.

My boy. My son.

My stomach flips. I've been numb all week. In a stupor, really. I hardly remember how I filled the hours until I could drive back to see them.

But I'm not fit to be a dad. Or be a decent mate. Not the kind Denali deserves. I'm nothing but a shell of a male with an animal I can barely control.

For the fortieth time, I survey the park for dangers, cataloging every person, every piece of equipment that might cause injury.

Denali approaches, stopping a few feet away from me. She texted me the address for this park. I guess she didn't want me to come to her place again, and I gotta respect that.

I notice she stands between me and the boy. She hasn't introduced us yet. I arrived and sat down to observe. I'm not sure I even want to be introduced. She doesn't want him to know I'm his dad.

Even while I know that's for the best, my lion roars with the injustice of it.

*Mine. My cub. My mate.*

But I can't claim them. And I sure as hell don't want to scare Denali off. She's protective of the boy—and rightly so.

"He's smart," I say to Denali.

"Yeah," she agrees.

"How..." My question trails off. I have no idea where to begin, what to ask.

She squats down. "I knew I'd conceived a few days after we... you know. Soon after I saw my chance to escape and took it. I've been on the run ever since."

I swallow. When Data-X took her from her home in New Orleans, they killed her pride—her grandfather and aunt. She's had no one since she escaped. She had this cub... alone.

Of all the unforgivable things I've done, leaving her pregnant and alone tops the list. It doesn't matter that I was a prisoner. I was supposed to protect. The guilt eats my lion alive.

"When I heard the lab burned down, I thought it was safe. I couldn't run forever. Nolan needed stability."

So she put down roots that allowed Sam to find her. "You were still hiding from me."

"Not exactly." She stops and blows out her breath. "I think I hoped you'd survive. That one day you'd meet him."

"And then what?" I stare at her, wondering what she'll

say. If there's a place for me in her and her son's life. If there is, would I want it? Am I even fit to consider it?

She hesitates, glancing back at the curly-headed boy. "My priority is Nolan. I'd do anything to keep him happy and safe."

And there it is. The reason I should never have sought Denali out or come here. My life, my animal is the opposite of safe.

My phone buzzes, breaking the silence. I rise. "I've got to take this."

"Nash, it's Parker."

"Yeah?" I don't have a fight scheduled for a few days, so I don't know what he wants.

"We're in Tucson. Something happened."

"What?" I don't know why the fuck he's reporting to me like I'm his alpha. Unless they need my help, in which case they're calling the wrong guy.

"The fight got busted. They took one of the fighters into custody."

I don't have time for this drama. I'm in a park watching a child who carries my genes. "Why are you telling me this?" I snap.

"There was a government agent behind it. He was shifter—or at least part shifter. And Nash—he asked about the labs."

"Fuck." The ground beneath me tilts.

"I just thought you should know. If Sam was able to find your mate, this guy might be able to, too."

*No.*

I can't have my mate exposed. My mate and her child.

Unacceptable.

I hang up without saying goodbye and stalk back, grinding my teeth.

Denali tenses, like she knows I'm trouble. I blink back my lion. "You need to move," I say immediately.

She jerks around, looking over both shoulders.

"There's a government agent hunting down shifters. If I found you, so can they."

Her eyes flash blue-grey, her lioness showing. "Where?"

"He picked up a shifter in Tucson. Asked him about the lab."

"Okaaaay. Doesn't sound like they're on my trail."

"No, but you can't risk it. You need to get out of here. You can stay with me." Even as I say it, I'm cursing the state of the hovel I've been living in. It's definitely not worthy of Denali and her son.

"I don't know, Nash. I just got settled. I've built up a little business. Nolan loves his preschool."

A rush of shame runs through me. My mate has been working her ass off as a single mother. I should be providing for them.

I shove my hands in my pockets. "Okay. Then I'm staying here. You require protection."

Her eyes narrow. "I don't know..."

I don't give a shit if she wants my protection or not, she's getting it. But I understand she doesn't want me around her cub. She's not ready for that. I hold up my hand. "I'll keep out of your way. I promise." Maybe I can find a place to move into close by. Or I'll get a fucking tent and pitch it on the hill behind her property. It's not like I haven't lived in a tent before. I had five tours in Iraq and Afghanistan.

She gives a non-committal nod, gaze sliding back to the little boy in the sandbox. The boy is casting us similar glances.

"You want to meet him?"

My heart thuds. *No.* Yes. Fuck, I don't know. I hate that I don't already know my kid. And I also think Denali is smart not to throw the door wide and let me in. I have nothing to offer my cub. Nothing but heartache and pain.

A frown appears between Denali's brows.

"Yeah." I clear my throat. "Definitely."

"Okay. Come on." She heads toward the sandbox. I follow a foot behind, checking the park again for anyone suspicious. It's empty.

The boy stops what he's doing, but doesn't get up, just peers up at me, his light brown curls falling across his eyes.

"Nolan, this is, um, a friend of mine. His name is Mr. Nash."

"Just Nash," I correct. I squat down. "Hey, Nolan."

Nolan's nostrils flare, probably because he's caught scent of my lion.

"Yeah, I'm like you and your mom," I confirm. Then I realize *mom* sounds wrong. Too old for a kid his age. What does he call her? *Momma? Mommy?* These are things I should know.

He drops his attention back to his sandcastle, tamping the wet sand down.

I've never felt so at a loss. "What are you making?"

The boy doesn't look up. "It's a robocar. A car that drives itself. Momma wants one so she doesn't have to deal with traffic."

*Momma.* Now I know.

I can't stop the smile as Denali ducks her head and shrugs. It's such a tiny, but sweet glimpse into their lives. I picture Denali driving Nolan through town, telling him all the things she wishes for.

The thought actually makes my chest ache. I want to be privy to all her fantasies—even if they're as benign as a self-driving car. The memory of what we did the last time I was here rushes back and my cock thickens.

Down, boy. Not here. Not in front of her kid. Our kid. Why is that hard for me to accept?

Maybe because I know nothing about children. Or because the cub is a stranger. Or because I'm not going to take on the father role with him. And that thought sets up an itchiness that crawls over every inch of my skin.

Am I going to allow some *other* asshole to take the role of a father with him?

Over my dead, fucking body.

"I've never seen another lion," the boy says, still not looking up from his work in the sand.

"Yeah, I haven't seen any, either. I've never even seen your momma's lion," I admit. The longing to see her animal grabs me like a fist closing around my shirt, tugging me forward into the depths of desire.

It's an unfamiliar desire. Do I want to mate her in animal form? According to Parker, only same-species shifters can engage that way, which was why he and Declan were the subjects of cross-gene therapy under Dr. Smyth's study.

Fuck, yes. I want it. Or at least I want the chase. The hunt. I want to run with her, take her down to her back and hold her throat with my teeth to demand her surrender. Then shift and fuck her beautiful body in human form. Because, damn. I would never grow tired of looking at that perfection.

Denali drags her lower lip through her teeth and I wonder if she's thinking of something similar.

*Denali*

. . .

Twenty minutes with Nash and all I can think about is how to get horizontal with him again. But I can't. Nolan's around all weekend. I'm not going to invite Nash in or to sleep over with Nolan in the house.

Not until...

I don't know.

I'm scared of the depth of my attraction to this guy I know very little about. It's not that I think he'd ever harm me or Nolan. Not like that.

But I have to be careful. Emotionally.

I don't want Nolan getting attached to someone if things aren't going to work out permanently. I don't want his heart broken.

Hell, I don't want my heart broken, either. And even though I was the one who did the leaving last time, Nash still took a chunk out of my heart.

Otherwise, he wouldn't have been haunting my dreams all this time, would he?

He cages his hands together and I eye the taut cords of his forearms, the golden hairs curling and glinting in the sun. His tattoos peek from beneath his short sleeves. Beautiful man.

Yeah, I want to see his lion, too.

"What about your parents?" Nolan asks Nash. "Didn't you see their lions?"

I still for the story, needing to know more about Nash. "My parents weren't around when I was young." The tightness in his tone tells me there's a story there. "I grew up in foster care. I never even met my own lion until Afghanistan..." he trails off and I sense he wants to shield

Nolan from the terrible things he's seen in his lifetime. I understand because I have to do it all the time.

"Mr. Nash was a soldier in the war, Nolan. A hero for our country. His lion came out in the war to save him."

Nolan puts down his shovel and looks Nash square in the eye for the first time. "Are lions heroes?"

Pain flickers over Nash's face.

I sit cross-legged beside him. "Yes." I speak over whatever answer Nash was going to give. Or whatever he's thinking. I don't like that tortured look in Nash's eye. He probably has more PTSD than I can even imagine.

"You know the lion is king of the jungle, right baby?"

Nolan won't look away from Nash. "Are you a mountain lion?"

A surprised laugh comes from Nash. "No. Jungle lion."

"I thought all lions had dark skin."

"Ah." Nash looks at me, surprise flitting over his face, like he's never considered why he's white. "Well, yeah. I suppose you're right—lions come from Africa. I guess my ancestors bred with humans or other shifters in America and gradually their skin got lighter. Just like your skin is lighter than your momma's."

"Yep, and mine is lighter than my daddy's," I supply. Nolan and I have discussed this before, but I never explained it in terms of breeding. I didn't want him wondering about the color of his father. I'd just told him different lions were different colors. I don't know where he got it in his head that lions should have dark skin. Of course, he's right. The only lion shifters I knew before Nash were of African descent.

"Smart kid," Nash mutters and my mouth twists in a wry smile.

"Yep." I hope this doesn't prompt questions from Nolan about who I bred with to get him. I fear it will.

"Are you my dad?"

*Shit!*

Way too smart for his own good.

Nash nearly falls over where he was squatting. He makes a show of sitting on his ass and brushing sand away before he answers, "No."

The single syllable sounds choked and gruff. I can tell it doesn't sit well with Nash to lie to our child, but I'm grateful he honored our agreement.

Even though the disappointment on Nolan's face kills me.

Nolan gets up and runs for the swings, like he wants to get away from Nash. Or hide. He's too little to climb up by himself, but he doesn't ask for help, just catches the seat and swoops around with it, his little feet dragging behind in the sand.

Nash stands up. For a moment I think he's going to leave, and I'm half disappointed, half relieved, but instead he walks over to the swings.

"Want me to push you?"

"No." Nolan sounds sullen.

"You sure?" he asks with mock incredulity. "Because I give the best pushes in the whole entire world. You haven't heard of me?"

He's captured Nolan's attention, but our son is still sulky. "No."

"Well, I give underdogs, overdogs. High-flyers, low-flyers. Side-flyers. You probably don't even know what all those are, do you?"

Nolan shakes his head, but he stands up from where he was dragging his knees around in the sand.

"Want to try?"

Nolan shrugs.

"How about this—you give it a try and tell me how you like it, and if it's not fun, you can get off. Okay?"

Nolan reaches for the chains and Nash lifts him up to sit on the plastic seat. "Now, tell me—do you like to go high?"

"Yes."

Nash is careful, pulling back the swing without dumping Nolan out the front of it. "Hang on tight."

I start to move toward them, to stop Nash from sending him too high, but Nash tosses a wink over his shoulder and lets Nolan go gently.

Oh lordy. The male is pure sex when the charm is turned on.

"Higher!" Nolan shouts.

Nash catches him around the waist, keeping him steady on the swing and pushes again. Nolan sails higher, kicking his little feet with glee.

I smile, my shoulders relaxing. This is just exactly how I always imagined Nash as a father—capable, protective, *sweet*.

Not as the broken male sitting on the park bench when I arrived. Nolan brings out the best in him. Well, I understand that. He's brought out the best in me, too. He's taught me love, trust, joy. Vulnerability.

I'd be a bitch to keep that from Nash. To keep him from Nash.

But he's also my baby. It's my job to protect him. I need to proceed with extreme caution.

Nash keeps pushing Nolan, so much longer than I ever have patience for. Nolan shrieks, "higher!" and each time Nash takes him a little higher, all the while showing the care for safety that keeps me from interfering.

Finally, in the interest of rescuing Nash, who's done more than any normal parent would ever do, I intercede. "Okay, baby, let's give Nash a rest."

"No!" Nolan cries, kicking his legs. "Higher!"

Nash catches Nolan around the waist and jogs forward with the swing to bring him to a stop. "You heard your momma." His voice is more cajoling than scolding and something catches in my chest. It's that longing again.

A mate who backs me up as a parent.

Nash shoves his hands in his pockets, stealing a glance at me.

He wants more. Of course he does.

Can I? Should I?

"I'm hungry," Nolan announces.

I pull some goldfish crackers out of my purse, and Nolan takes them.

"Well... thanks for inviting me," Nash says. "I should get going."

I'm surprised he's making this easy for me. He's leaving it open to end the playdate with our son and walk away.

But it feels wrong. Every cell in my body wants to be closer to Nash right now. To get up and personal with him. Invite him home. Take his clothes off. Blow his mind with my mouth on his cock, just to thank him for being so cool with Nolan.

But I know one thing. A dominant lion like Nash doesn't back down easily. So if he's giving me this window of opportunity, I need to take it.

"Yeah, it was nice," I manage to say as I scoop Nolan up to carry on my hip.

Something akin to pain ripples over Nash's face, but then it's gone again, before I can guess what it's about.

"Um, will I see you—"

"You will." The utter assurance in his voice sends a shiver up my spine. I sense a promise or a vow under his words, but I can't decipher it. He's planning something.

Which should cause me worry, but that's not the emotion skittering through my body.

No. It's excitement.

Nash hasn't stopped coming for me.

And he probably won't.

Ever.

And my lioness is purring over it.

# 6

# N *ash*

SUNRISE OVER TEMECULA IS BEAUTIFUL. So different than San Diego, where the fog tucks in around the coast. I watch it light up the golden hill where I slept behind Denali's place, casting pink rays against her little cottage and the vineyards below.

Her older neighbor comes out on her porch with her coffee and I go still, so I won't attract any attention.

My body aches from spending the night on the hard ground without any blankets, but the satisfaction of having watched over my mate and cub trumps all else. I don't care if I have to spend the rest of my life sleeping on rocks, if it keeps them safe, I'll do it.

I look back down the hill. Denali's neighbor has moved inside. I stand up and stretch, then creep a little closer to the cottage. I have to admit, I'm hoping for a glimpse of Denali or Nolan. I may be keeping a respectful distance, but that doesn't mean I'm not still drawn like a magnet to them. I want to know everything about them—their daily routines, what they eat for breakfast, what television shows they watch.

Movement catches my eye and I see the neighbor's back on the porch, holding a shotgun. She fires before I can even think.

It's a warning shot. At least I hope it is. It ricochets off a rock nearby and sends me charging down the hill. "Hey!" I shout at the same time she yells, "Hold it right there."

I force myself to slow my pace from a run to a brisk stride as I continue to advance. No one shoots a gun off near my family. Not even sixty-year-old ladies wearing flower print gardening smocks.

Denali flies out of her cottage and I snarl at seeing her out, unprotected. My mate requires no protection, though. She takes in her neighbor, then whips around to see me.

Surprisingly, my lion doesn't want to bleed her. I don't feel that familiar violence rising up in me. Only the need to protect. Which in this case, requires me to be calm. "Put the gun down," I order in my best alpha voice. Turns out, it doesn't matter, because Denali has already sprinted to her neighbor's and snatched the gun from her hands. I half expect her to turn it on me and cock it, but she empties the barrel before hurling the shotgun into the flowerbed.

When she turns to face me, her eyes are lion-bright and she's breathing hard.

And damn. She's wearing the thinnest t-shirt imaginable and those tiny shorts that make her legs look six miles long. She puts her hands on her hips. "What in the hell is going on?"

"Is this him?" the older woman demands as I stride up.

Even though the gun's out of her hands, she still looks prepared to murder me if she has to.

I would take offense, except Denali appears baffled. "Who?"

"The one you been hidin' from. Is this the boy's father?"

Her words hit me like a punch to the gut, but Denali's response doesn't fit. She splutters, "No! Well—it's complicated. But regardless, why were you shooting at him?"

"I saw him sneaking around your place. Looks like he's been there all night." She turns her narrowed gaze on me. Her eyes are flinty grey to match the steel of her personality. "Were you there all night?"

I nod. No sense in lying. I direct my gaze at Denali. "I can't leave you unprotected."

Denali's gaze warms, but she steps forward and slaps my chest. "Stupid male. You scared the crap out of me and Mrs. Davenfield. And what? You just slept out on the hill? Under the open sky?"

I can't stop the lazy grin. "Stars were beautiful, but not nearly as beautiful as you in those little—"

She cuts me off with another slap to my chest. "All right, Romeo. Let's get you inside and fed." She steers me off her neighbor's wooden porch. "I'm sorry, Mrs. Davenfield. Nothing to worry about. Nash is safe. He's just worried about someone else showing up and hassling me."

"And I'm worried about crazy neighbors with shotguns," I mutter under my breath as we walk away.

"You should be," Mrs. Davenfield calls to my back. Apparently, her hearing is as sharp as her eyesight. "Sneaking around people's property at five in the morning is a shootable offense around here."

"I'll keep that in mind, ma'am."

"Looks like you're the type who knows how to handle a gun, himself."

I turn to get a better look at Mrs. Davenfield, grateful Denali has her as a watchful neighbor. Not much gets past this woman.

Denali loops her hand through my elbow and tugs me forward. "Come on, Nash. I'll make you breakfast. You like Canadian bacon?"

My stomach grumbles. "Love it." I'm surprised at how intense a pleasure it is to have Denali offer to cook for me. I'm suddenly hard as a rock and wondering if Nolan is still in bed.

The minute we're inside her door, I snake an arm around her waist and pull her back up against my straining cock. My teeth graze her shoulder. "Promise me something," I rumble in her ear.

Her sweet cinnamon scent fills the air. "What?" Her voice is husky.

I slip my hand between her legs and cup her mons. "Don't ever go outside your house dressed like this again."

"Or what?" There's a taunt in her voice and it sends my desire into overdrive.

I slide one hand up to squeeze her breast while I stroke my fingers over the seam of her shorts, pressing it into her slit.

"I'll have to kill any male who looks at you, for one thing."

Her head falls back on my chest and she rocks her hips forward, pushing into my hand.

"And then I'd have to punish you for making me crazy with jealousy."

She brings her hand to cover mine, directing my fingers to push harder over her clit. "Oh yeah?"

Damn. The husk in her voice nearly blinds me with lust. But Nolan must be sleeping just a few feet away.

"Let's get in the shower," Denali suggests. Smart female. The sound of the water will drown out her cries.

I propel her forward, not removing my hands from her beautiful body. We jostle into the bathroom and strip our clothes off in record time. She turns to get in and I smack her ass with a loud crack.

"Shh." She tosses a smile over her shoulder as she climbs in and everything in me lights up.

It's not just passion—although there's a mountain of that. I'm also filled with an exuberance, God, maybe even *joy*. Everything about this moment with Denali fills me up. Sets me free.

It's like my whole life, I've been waiting for this point in time, when I get to laugh and play with my mate. Fuck her senseless. Eat breakfast with her afterward.

I can't believe the intense pleasure of it.

I step into the shower after her, rolling a condom on my erection. I want to take my time. Soap her, wash her hair.

But it's an impossibility.

I flatten her against the wall, and my hands cup her ass. Water soaks us, streams down her face, wetting her eyelashes and lips. Even with it, her scent fills the room, sending me into animal drive.

My kiss is hard and demanding. My tongue sweeps into her mouth, teeth bump teeth.

Her legs lift to hook around my waist and my cock is right where I want it to be. I don't even have to use my hand to guide it in. I find her entrance and push forward, filling her with a powerful thrust.

She gasps and clutches my shoulders.

"Are you okay, beautiful?"

"Uhn." She rubs her tits against my torso, the hard points of her nipples dragging through my chest hair. Her hips snap against mine, urging me deeper.

"You want more, baby?"

"I want it, Nash," she breathes in my ear.

I lose all control then, helplessly pumping into her. She rocks to meet my thrusts, taking me deeper, meeting and matching my rhythm.

"Nash."

Every time I hear my name on her lips, I go wilder. A growl starts up in my chest.

She slaps her hand over my mouth to stop it from coming out, all the while riding my cock, her beautiful tits bouncing and swaying.

I slip one hand between her ass cheeks to press against her back hole and she makes a desperate sound. Her arms tangle around my neck, and she uses them to leverage herself faster, taking me even deeper.

I massage her anus as I plow into her and she comes, her head thrown back, mouth open on a silent scream.

The squeeze of her muscles around my cock sends me hurtling to my own finish. I fuck her hard and fast, the slap of our wet bodies echoing against the tile until I, too, reach climax and come.

The satisfaction is cellular. My entire body flushes with it and yet, as I ease out, it's still not enough.

I want to claim her again.

And again.

But I can't right now. I settle for kissing her wet, open mouth. "I would sleep a thousand nights on your rocky hill if it meant this was my reward every morning."

She ducks her head, blushing and steps out of the shower. I feel her loss acutely, but I take a moment to do a quick soap lather and rinse before I turn off the water and get out.

When I come out, she has a towel wrapped around her and her hands on her hips. "You can't sleep out on that hill, Nash."

My jaw sets. "I'm watching over you." I say it with finality. Nothing will budge me from this. She's my mate. She has a cub. They are mine to protect until the end of my days.

She rolls her eyes and shakes her head before she leaves the bathroom, but I have a feeling she knows she can't change my mind.

I pull on my clothes and step out at the same time she exits her bedroom wearing a short, flowered dress.

I growl my approval, earning an upward tilt of her lips.

She heads to the kitchen and starts pulling out food. "You make the coffee, I'll make the food."

I nod and get to work, all the while admiring her ease in the kitchen. Thank fuck she's a shifter. She knows how much I eat. She opens two packages of Canadian bacon and fries the slabs of meat up at the same time she whisks together pancake mix and sets the table.

"Good morning, bud," Denali chirps when Nolan appears in the kitchen.

He scoots behind his mother's leg, playing shy while watching me. I long to tousle his curls and tickle the shyness right out of him, but I don't want to overstep.

"Nash came over for breakfast. Want to help me make his pancakes?"

The little boy nods and she pulls a stepstool over to the stove. Nolan climbs up on it to supervise. She gives him blueberries to drop into the pancake batter, helping him make a smiley face. I watch the two of them together, contentment coursing through my veins.

I could watch this for the rest of my life. Except I'd like to give Denali more cubs. A whole den of them.

I shake those aberrant thoughts out of my head. This picture of domesticity is doing something strange to me. I need to remember I don't belong here. My lion's a killer and he's not happy unless he's fighting. A shifter like that has no business being around children.

"How long is he staying, momma?" Nolan asks.

She darts a glance at me and clears her throat. "Um, just for breakfast, honey. He was just checking in on us to make sure we're safe, but now he knows we are."

A shard of glass pierces my chest and lodges right in my heart.

But I already knew not to get comfortable here.

I definitely don't belong with them.

~

*Denali*

I HAVE a smile on my face as I put away laundry that afternoon. I think it's been there all day. Even Nolan notices. "You're fun, momma," he said after I spun him around for the fifteenth time. "I like when you're happy."

I don't even want to think about what's made me so cheerful.

Morning sex with a lion?

Check.

Being watched over by a vigilant soldier who doesn't give a damn about his personal comfort?

Double-check.

Knowing he'll probably be there again tonight?

Yeah, triple check.

I can't let him sleep out on the hill again.

So what am I going to do? Let him in? Invite him to stay?

The thought sends my heart skittering into overdrive. But what will I tell Nolan? How long before he gets attached?

I find it fascinating that once again, my animal instincts didn't alert me to his presence. A shifter creeping around outside my cottage and I slept like a baby. In fact, I think I rested better last night than I have in years. It's like my lioness knew he was on watch and I could finally let my guard down.

I let Nolan fill the loneliness that ate at me after I escaped Data-X. I made myself believe I didn't want or need anyone else. But I do.

My phone rings. I check the screen. Mrs. Davenfield. My landlady and nosy neighbor. I sigh. She probably wants to talk about why Nash was hanging around this morning.

"Hi, Mrs. Davenfield."

"He's out front."

"Excuse me?"

"Nolan's dad. Sitting in a car watching the house."

I curse, but there's no upset behind it. In fact, I think my smile's grown bigger. "Okay, thanks for letting me know."

"Want me to call the cops?"

"No, no. Definitely not. He's not a danger. And Mrs. Davenfield?"

"What is it, hon?"

I peek into the living room where Nolan is watching his favorite show, *Curious George,* on the television and lower my voice. "Um, don't say that in front of Nolan, 'kay? He doesn't know."

"O-kaaay." She drags out the last syllable like she's hoping I'll elaborate, but I ignore it.

"Thanks," I say and hang up before she can ask any questions.

I head outside, an extra swing to my hips as I stride over to Nash's beat-up Mustang. The windows are down, and his lids drop to half-mast as he watches me.

I lean into his window, catching his chin when his gaze drops to my cleavage. "Still keeping an eye on my place?" There's a purr in my voice. A seductive quality I don't even recognize. I never knew I had a temptress in me.

Nash flashes that wicked grin. The one he wore before he spanked me yesterday. My pussy clenches. "Right now, I'm keeping my eye on you," he drawls.

"Mm hmm. Like what you see?"

"You know I do."

"Well, you might as well come in. I can't have you sitting out here in your car or Mrs. Davenfield will get her shotgun again."

"Yes, she's had her eye on me. I have to say, I don't mind you having a protective neighbor."

My chest squeezes. He genuinely cares about keeping us safe. As a mate should. Nolan must've followed me out, because he races toward us now, barreling into my leg and holding it.

"Can you say hi to Nash?" I prompt.

Nash puts out his fist.

Nolan looks at it, confused.

"Fist bump? Put your hand out." Nolan complies, and Nash gently touches large knuckles to Nolan's, then taps the top of his fist with his.

Nolan grins and punches Nash's fist as hard as he can.

"Nolan!" I'm shocked to see my sweet little boy acting aggressive, but Nash loves it.

"Oh you want to tussle?" He scoops our shrieking son up and tickles him.

My chest fills with gooey warmth.

The moment he puts him down, Nolan yells, "More!" and they keep at it while I head to the kitchen to grab us all a glass of fresh squeezed lemonade with basil in it.

∼

*Nash*

The sound of Nolan's laughter does something peculiar to my heart—makes it contract and expand at the same time.

I toss and tickle him until he collapses on the floor, half-moaning, half-laughing.

"Okay," Denali soothes. "Who wants some lemonade?"

"I do, I do!" Nolan yells, racing forward to take his plastic cup with a lid and straw.

Denali hands me a glass filled with ice and a clear liquid with green herbs floating in it. I take a sip and savor the zing of lemon and some other taste.

"Mmm—what is this?"

"It's my version of lemonade. I don't like Nolan to have too much sugar, so I make it with fresh lemons, stevia, and a little basil."

I gape at her. Smoking hot single mom is also managing to pull a Martha Stewart existence? I drink the refreshing liquid down in three gulps and smack my lips. "That was the best thing I've ever tasted."

She beams at me. "I'll get you some more."

My phone rings and I pull it out. Parker.

"Hey Alpha," Declan sings out in a lilting brogue.

"Not your alpha," I mumble for the gazillionth time, watching Nolan pretend not to watch me as he plays with a little train set on the coffee table. I crouch down to help him fix where the track has come apart as a queasy feeling moves through me. Who am I kidding, interacting with this kid? I'm not even fit to be alpha to a bunch of fucked up shifters—how fucking far does that make me from being fit as a dad?

"Did you find her?"

I glance back at Denali, coming in with a fresh glass of lemonade. Her long, sleek legs and elegant line of bare neck make the most mundane movements graceful. "Yeah."

A cheer greets my words. Not just Declan—it sounds like a roomful of people.

"And? How'd it go?" Parker chimes in.

"You're on speaker," Declan informs me.

I pinch the bridge of my nose with a thumb and forefinger. Fuck, my head hurts.

"Alpha? Alpha?"

"Not your alpha," I growl. Denali shoots me a worried glance and I turn away. I've got to get my animal under control.

"You're in Temecula, right?"

"Yeah," I answer just as Parker adds, "We're close. We're coming to see her."

"What? No—"

"It's a party," Declan crows.

Laurie says in the background. "Can we order pizza?"

"No. Stay where you are," I order with all the force I can muster.

"Sorry, no can do. Alpha mojo doesn't work over the phone. Yell at us in person all you want," Parker says,

"He won't yell at us," Declan reasons. "He wants to impress his mate."

"We'll be there in ten."

"How do you know where I am?"

"Laurie bugged your phone," Parker says.

"See ya soon, Alpha!" Declan shouts and the call goes dead.

Fuck.

"Everything all right?" Denali stands a few steps away, her brow furrowed. I resist the urge to throw the phone and curse.

"Fine. Just... we're about to get company. Not like that," I add when she tenses. "Friends of mine. Housemates actually."

"They called you *Alpha.*"

Fucking shifter hearing.

"I'm not their alpha. They're not even lions. They're not fit to be a pack anyway—bunch of rejects. Leftovers from the Data-X experiments."

She pales. "I see." When she darts a worried glance at Nolan, the fist in my solar plexus tightens.

"He's safe, Denali. I give you my word." For what it's worth.

She nods, once, and the tightness eases when I realize she believes me.

Twenty minutes later, a white Camaro roars up. I step out onto the porch and Denali and Nolan follow me.

"Brace yourself," I mutter as Parker, Declan, and Laurie make their way to us. Someone says something to Declan to set him off, because he starts mock punching his companions.

"Not now," Parker shoves the Irishman into Laurie. The tall, long limbed shifter's glasses go flying and he almost keels over.

"All right, Jay-sus." Declan grabs Laurie and helps him retrieve his glasses. "I'll behave."

"This is your pack?" Denali asks in disbelief.

"Not mine." I shake my head.

"Parker." I point as the grey-headed guy approaches. My fight manager stops in his tracks, but Declan and Laurie keep going, almost bowling him over.

"Declan." I jab the air, pointing each one out. "Laurie Lawrence."

"It's like the three stooges," Denali murmurs as Parker turns on Declan and Laurie pretends to bash their heads together. "Only one is thin."

"And they're shifters," I agree with a sigh.

Denali sniffs the air, her eyes glinting with her lioness. "What are they?"

"Parker's a wolf. Well, mostly wolf. Laurie's a... well, you'll figure it out. He's pretty shy. I'm not sure what Declan is."

"I'm Irish," Declan offers, grinning wide, showing off crooked canines.

"I'm an owl," Laurie raises his hand with a sheepish smile. His head twitches like he's being electrocuted.

Denali sucks in a breath and the scent of cinnamon fills the air.

"Lioness." Parker eyes her with satisfaction.

A growl rumbles through me, and I move closer to Denali.

"Mom?" says a small voice around our knees. "I thought we couldn't talk about our animals."

Denali whirls, crouching to grip her son's shoulders.

"That's right baby. That's safest. Go inside and play now, while momma talks to Nash's friends."

Nolan trundles back inside, but the three newcomers got a good look at him. Parker and Laurie's mouths hang wide open.

Declan makes a choking sound. "Holy fecking—"

"Stop swearing," I growl. "No foul language, no inappropriate topics. Understand?"

Laurie nods vigorously, eyes huge behind his thick glasses.

"Is that...?" Parker points and I swat his hand. The boy isn't a freak show. Nolan still watches us through the screen door, curiosity written on his face. A bunch of strange guys showing up to ogle him—this kid is gonna be traumatized.

"He looks just like you," Laurie murmurs.

I can't help whirling to see if it's true. On further study, the line of Nolan's jaw, his nose, the gold tints in his hair—he does look like me.

My organs seem to shift and rearrange inside me.

"Nash? What's going on?" Parker asks.

"This is Denali. My mate."

She shakes off my hand. "Our mating doesn't count," she tells the crew. "It happened under duress."

My lion growls again.

Parker sniffs the air, which is tinged with our mingled spice scent. No shifter can come close to Denali and not know I've marked her. "I think it still counts."

"It's complicated," I say, and Denali shoots me a grateful look.

"Understood," Declan says. "For a simple soldier, Nash is pretty complicated."

I glare at him to no effect.

"How did you all meet?" Denali asks.

"Cage fighting," Parker says. "Shifter style."

I curse at Denali's shocked look. This is not how I wanted to break the news to her.

"His lion needs to bleed someone on a regular basis. Almost nightly now, isn't it?" Declan continues blithely.

"Shut up."

"I'm Parker, ma'am," Parker extends a hand. "Manager at The Pit. I arrange Nash's fights."

"And Laurie and I bet on them," Declan says. "We're bookies, too. Your mate's made us a lot of money over the past few months."

"I see. And you're his pack?"

"He's our alpha even though he says he's not," Laurie says.

"How does that work?" Denali's brow wrinkles.

"We call him Alpha and he tells us to feck off—hey!" Declan breaks off as Laurie elbows him in the ribs.

"Don't swear," the gawky shifter reminds him.

"All right, all right, birdbrain. Jay-sus, your elbows are like daggers." Grimacing, Declan rubs his chest where Laurie jabbed him.

"Who wants dinner?" Parker rubs his hands together. "Pizza?"

I clear my throat just as Denali says "Actually—"

"Pizza, momma?" Nolan pops out from behind her. "Can I have pizza?"

Denali sighs.

"O' course, little cub," Declan declares. "Ya can have all the pizza ya want. What?" he pulls an innocent face as all but Nolan glare at him.

An hour later, we're sitting in Denali's living room, ten empty pizza boxes stacked on the porch. Shifters eat a lot. Declan and Parker fight over the last slice.

"So you two only met once before?" Laurie asks. He lounges on the floor, his long form stretched out where he's been playing with Nolan for the past twenty minutes. He isn't twitching so badly.

"Yes," Denali says. She and I share a couch, and every nerve in me is alive, wanting to scoot a few inches to the right and touch her.

"You probably want some time alone then," Parker speaks up.

"Aye, that's a grand idea," Declan says. "We can babysit—"

"No," Denali and I almost shout together.

"All right," Declan puts his hands up. "Jay-sus. Ya think I offered to feck—"

"No swearing," Laurie and Parker both admonish. Parker slaps Declan's head.

"No hitting either," Denali adds.

Muttering, Declan tromps out to the porch.

I rub my forehead. "I'm just grateful he didn't bring his hooch."

"Oh, he brought it," Laurie says. "We just wouldn't let him bring it into the house."

"Go keep an eye on him," I order. Laurie follows him.

Denali rises and reaches for Nolan. "All right baby, time for bed."

"But I'm not sleepy," the boy says with a yawn.

"I know." She herds him to the hall, pausing a moment to glance back at me, a question in her eyes.

"I'll wait for you," I say. After a moment of hesitation, she nods.

For a while I sit and listen to her getting Nolan ready for bed. His high voice protesting, her beautiful murmur.

Simple, domestic sounds that should put me at ease. I rub my eyes. What the hell am I doing here?

As I head to the porch, I realize my lion is still quiet. He's been that way since I bedded Denali. For once he's relaxed, but I know it's only a matter of time before the flashbacks return. Before my lion needs to make someone bleed.

"Good mate you got there, boss," Parker says as I head over to the white Camaro. He and Declan are smoking. A flask sits by Declan.

"Gotta fight tomorrow at The Pit," the wolf adds. "You want me to move it?"

Trying to think of an answer, I stare at the slope behind her house, where I chased and conquered her. I've lived so long with my lion rampaging, I don't know any other life.

"We should go." Declan hops off the car hood, tossing his cigarette to the ground. "You and the missus got a lot of stuff to work out."

Understatement. As the guys pile into the car, I clench my fists. Usually, they're torn up from a fight. All healed now. Usually that's my cue to return to The Pit and pound someone until I don't feel anything.

Shifter fights, flashbacks, and an unstable lion. What life can I possibly offer a mate and a son?

"We'll see you tomorrow," Parker says. "Unless we don't." A half wave, and they pull out of the drive, and I realize as much as I pretended to resent their visit, the messed-up crew of shifters was the only thing distracting me from my problem.

∼

*Denali*

. . .

"Are your friends going to spend the night? Like a sleepover?"

"No, baby."

"That's too bad. They were nice. Especially the bird-one." Adorable in footie pajamas, Nolan climbs into bed. I scoot behind him to read him a story. He insists on reading parts of the book himself, and I take the chance to cuddle him and breathe in the baby shampoo scent clinging to his curls. I used to fall asleep like this, coming in after a day in the fields where I worked with the other migrant workers, relieving the babysitter and taking the precious moments to hold my boy.

Does Nash even realize what it's been like, raising a son and trying to survive? My lioness is ready to be with him, but it'll take more than an afternoon at a playground and a pizza dinner for him to prove to me he should be a part of my son's life.

"Momma," Nolan asks in a sleepy voice, "is Nash my dad?"

I try not to stiffen. "What makes you say that?"

"Laurie said I look like him."

I take a big breath and pray Nolan falls asleep in the next two seconds.

"Is he?"

I swallow down the lump in my throat. I don't want to tell him. Don't want his little heart to be broken like mine was if things don't work out between Nash and me. But I can't lie. I asked Nash to and it didn't sit right with me. "Yes, sweetie. He is. He was off fighting for our country and he never knew I had you, otherwise he would've been here for you." That's pretty close to the truth. Fighting for his life, not his country, but it was his country's fault.

"Is he going to stay with us?"

"I don't know yet. Nash and momma are still trying to figure things out."

"I want a dad."

I suck in a breath at the sudden pain. I thought I was doing fine by my son, being a mom and a dad for him. I guess I was wrong. "I know, baby," I squeeze him tighter. "We'll see what happens. In the meantime, momma loves you. You know that, right?"

"Yeah." He pauses a moment, and adds, "I love you, momma."

"That's what matters. I'm not going anywhere."

∼

*Nash*

The scent of cinnamon hits the room before Denali. I rise from the couch, brushing crumbs from my shirt.

"You're still here."

"I told you I'd wait for you," I say. "Besides, you didn't offer me dessert." I lift the lid off the cookie jar and take another cookie.

"You're worse than Nolan."

"These are so good, I could eat them all. You want one?"

"Hell, yes." She leans against the counter and goes to grab the cookie I offer. I shake my head and bring it to her mouth. Blue-grey leaps into her eyes as she lets me feed it to her.

"These are your favorite, right? Peanut butter."

"Nolan's too, now. I make them all the time."

"He's a good kid."

Her face softens. "The best."

Slowly, I feed her another cookie. Her eyes dart over my face, filled with longing. There's a little furrow between her brow, though, when I'm done.

"Nash, what are we—"

I lower my head and stop her words with my kiss.

∽

*Denali*

"Favorite cookie?" *Nash asks. We both sit on the cot, picking at the food the guards sent in.*

*"Peanut butter."*

*Nash raises a brow. "Peanut butter cookies," he murmurs.*

*"They're easy to make, and almost every kitchen has the ingredients."*

*The door swings open and I slam my body back to the wall, fear crawling up my arms. What a cowardly, cringing creature I've become.*

*Nash does the opposite. I peer past his huge body as he faces the triangle of guards.*

*"You're supposed to breed her," one orders.*

*"I already did." Nash's mild voice is at odds with the violent tension in every muscle of his body. He had—after turning my body to molten lava with his tongue between my legs.*

*"Boss wants you to do it again." Two of the guards raise batons that crackle with electricity. I suppress a whimper and press myself further into the corner.*

*"You're upsetting her."*

*"We'll do more than that if you don't do as you're told. You both know what to do."*

*"Get out," Nash growls.*

*The guards are smart enough to keep their eyes glued to Nash. He's fearsome, even in human form. I'll bet his lion would make the guards pee themselves. They think they're invincible with their electric wands, though.* "You gonna do what you're supposed to, or should we do the job for you?" *The taunting guard unzips his pants.*

*A roar breaks from Nash's throat and he starts to charge. The first guard blanches and backs away, but his friends are all too ready to wade in with their shock sticks. Nash doesn't stand a chance.*

"Stop," *I scream and scramble to his side.* "Don't hurt him. We'll do it. Just…"

*Nash's shoulders heave with the exertion of keeping his lion in check. His eyes glow a lethal yellow.* "Leave us." *His voice is thick.* "Before I tear you apart."

"Get on with it," *the guard snaps, and the door slams shut.*

*Nash's head bows, his fists clenched at his side. So powerful. So helpless.*

*I've only known him a few hours, but I can't stand to see him like this.*

*I touch his shoulder.*

"Denali… I—"

"It's all right," *I stop his apology. It's not his fault. None of it is. I reach for him and run my hand down the hard line of his back, my body heating at the feel of the muscles bunched under my palm.*

"Thank you for protecting me."

*He turns, and I almost flinch at the fire burning in his eyes. He wants me. Again. I blink and let the lioness out. Desire pours through me in slow, heated waves.*

*Nash rumbles with approval—somewhere between a roar and a purr. He cups my nape and claims my mouth, his kiss hungry. Insistent. He's already used his clever tongue between my legs, brought me to orgasm and fit his length inside me. This time is different, though.*

*I realize now how much he'd held back before.*


NASH'S APPRECIATION for my cooking shouldn't please me so much. This isn't the 1950s. I'm not my grandmother, back in New Orleans, showing love through food. I never thought I'd want to win a man's heart through his stomach. But I love the way he acts like the simplest things I've made are a rare delicacy. Kinda how he treats me.

He claims my mouth, much like he did that first night, with a ferocity that makes my knees go weak. It's like he can't get enough of me. Or his very survival depends on keeping our lips locked.

That first night I suppose it did.

Maybe it still does—for Nash, anyway. His lion seems calmer, his bruises and cuts all healed.

There's a power to knowing I healed him.

I remember my grandmother used to say, "Don't ever use your lady parts for gain, Denali. They're for healing." I never realized she meant it literally.

Right now, I'm dying to give Nash another healing.

I nip his lower lip and work the button on his jeans.

"Careful, baby," he rasps. "You sure you want me off my leash?" He pulls my shirt off over my head.

I arch a brow at him. "Pretty sure I can handle you."

The corners of his mouth tilt into a lopsided smile. "I doubt it, baby." He backs me up against the kitchen counter and turns me to face it. When he grabs a wooden spoon from the utensil bin, my heart starts to thud with excitement. This is the side of Nash I crave. The dominant alpha taking charge.

As much as I appreciate his respect for my boundaries, in my dreams he never takes no for an answer. Never lets me push him away. He demands his rightful place in my life. But those are just fantasies.

Nash taps my ass lightly with the spoon. He's testing me. Waiting for a reaction.

I look over my shoulder at him. "Are you going to actually use that spoon, or should—"

He moves swiftly, pinning my hands behind my back and forcing my chest down on the counter. I laugh as he smarts my ass with the wooden spoon. I'm a shifter, so pain is fleeting. In this moment, it registers only as stimulus, augmenting my desire.

Nash nudges my feet wider. "Spread those long, lovely legs. Show me the place I'm going to make sore tonight."

I bare my teeth and growl at his dirty talk, my core turning molten.

Nash brings the spoon up between my legs, spanking my pussy. I jerk against his hold, not that I really want to be free. It's intense, but wonderful. Pain that blooms right away into pleasure.

"How do you think it will feel to take your mate's big lion cock after your pussy has been thoroughly spanked?"

I seriously don't know how I keep from passing out. I'm hot and dizzy with lust, frantic to get my shorts off. To remove all the barriers between us.

"Why don't you show me?" I dare.

He keeps spanking my pussy with firm taps of the wooden spoon. Then it suddenly clatters to the floor and he shoves my shorts and panties down my hips. "It's been *hours* since I last fucked this pussy," he says, like that's way too long. But I remember from our cell he had no shortage of stamina.

He releases my wrists to roll on a condom and I wriggle out of the shorts and panties tangled at my feet. I brace my hands against the kitchen counter and return to my position, feet spread wide, ass out.

Nash slaps my bare ass and I shush him. "Too loud," I murmur.

"Oh, it's going to be loud," he growls right before he impales me with his cock. He covers my mouth on the next thrust. "Because I definitely plan on making you scream."

My nipples scrape the inside of my bra, hard as diamonds. Nash wraps an arm around my hips to protect them from banging against the counter, all the while rocking me up to my toes with each savage thrust.

"You needed to be claimed by your mate, didn't you, baby? Did you need a big lion cock to fill you up?" This ungentlemanly side of him is so in contrast to the lion I mated with, yet it turns me on just as much. No—way more.

"Yes." My lips move against his hand.

I do need it. I need it so badly I'm ready to weep or beg for him to bring me to climax.

His thumb slips into my mouth and I suck on it, hard. He continues to ram into me, slapping my buttocks with his loins, lifting me to my toes with each powerful instroke. I want—no, I need—to take him deeper. Deeper than this position allows.

As if he senses that I'm restless, he pulls out and whirls me around. I cat-attack him—leaping to straddle his waist, arms wrapped around his neck. He stumbles back, eyes glowing with appreciation.

"You need to be on top, my queen?"

I bite his neck savagely. He hits the table and stumbles, then crashes to the floor, careful to keep me on top.

Satisfaction spreads through me. As much as I love

when he takes charge, a surge of power rushes through me with the roles reversed. I pin his arms down and he lets me, even though I know he could easily best me. I straddle his hips, lowering myself onto his stiff erection.

"Ride me, little lion. Show me how greedy you are for this cock." He thrusts his hips up and I gasp when he hits my inner walls.

I snarl as I slide over his thick manhood, dig my nails into his forearms. I grind my clit down on the base of his shaft each time I sweep up.

Nash pants, sweat gathering at his trimmed hairline, but he doesn't surrender to his own pleasure. He watches me intently, fascination playing over his expression. I feel beautiful. Feral. Wondrous. I've never disliked my life as a shifter, but I'm not sure I've reveled in it before. In this moment, I wouldn't trade who I am for anything.

A wild, dangerous beast in the body of a beautiful woman. I am glorious, sensuous power. I am victory.

I am queen of the jungle. Marked mate to Nash.

There's no denying our bond. Not when I feel what he does to my animal. How he sets me free. Our bodies were made for one another.

Fate may have brought us together in the worst possible way, but he's mine, and I'm his.

I throw back my head and clench my teeth down on a scream. The moment my muscles start to tighten around Nash's cock, he throws off my hold on his arms and grips my hips, yanking me down over his cock with enough force to split me.

My eyes roll back in my head at the sheer ecstasy of it. The satisfaction.

Nash closes his mouth breaking off his shout and jacks

his hips off the floor, lifting me into the air like I'm riding a bucking bronco.

A breathless laugh tumbles out of me when he collapses, limp, beneath me. I lower my head to kiss him.

∼

*Nash*

I caress her powerful legs, the tight curve of her ass. She does the same, running her palms down my pecs with an approving murmur.

"So strong. Fighting suits you."

"King of the Beasts," I say. "That's what they call me in the ring."

"King," her eyes light. "So that makes me your queen?"

Catching the nape of her neck, I draw her down for a kiss.

"Shhhh," she goes quiet and listens and I hold still, my cock still inside her. She relaxes and rocks against me. It's not Nolan. "Momma radar," she says with a little smile. "You get it at birth and wake up at the slightest noise every night for the rest of your life."

I consider this. Will I get some sort of similar dad ability? Or is it too late?

Then she rocks against me and I lose all ability to think.

"I told Nolan you're his dad."

I go perfectly still. In fact, I think my heart stops completely. "You did?" I sound choked.

"Yeah. He asked, and I just didn't feel right lying. I know I asked you not to tell him, and I appreciate you honoring my request. But you don't have to keep it secret anymore."

I still don't know how to breathe. "Yeah? What'd he say?"

"He asked me if you're going to live here."

I watch her face closely for signs of what she thinks. What she wants. She's hard to read. "It's my duty to protect you whether you choose to let me stay or not."

Her eyes narrow. "Are you here out of duty or desire?"

I grasp her hips and thrust my semi-hard cock inside her. "Do you have to ask?"

She's not having it. She shifts to the side and dismounts. "I mean for Nolan." She doesn't look at me when she says it.

My gut twists up in a knot. I climb to my feet and dispose of the condom.

*I don't fucking know.*

I don't know the answer to that question. I don't have a clue how to be a father. Before I chased them down, I was barely surviving.

"I want to do what's right by my son," I choke. That's the truth.

She folds her arms across her chest. "That's not the same thing," she snaps.

I hold my hands up. "Whoa. Whoa. I'm not saying I don't *want* to be a father to him. I do. Please remember I only found out about his existence a few days ago. If I'm not ready to pin the *Father of the Year* badge on it's because I don't have a fucking clue how to be that for him. That's all."

Her shoulders drop. "You're right. I understand. Forgive me, I'm just protective of Nolan."

I walk over and pull her into my arms. "Of course you are. I wouldn't expect anything else. We'll take things slow, okay? For now, I can sleep on the couch and guard you both. The rest we'll figure out."

She melts into me, wrapping her arms around my waist. "Thank you," she murmurs against my shirt.

I stroke her soft curls. "Thank you, baby. I'm just grateful you're letting me in the house. Not that I didn't love having your neighbor shoot at me."

She giggles and smiles up at me and I catch my breath and how fresh and beautiful she still looks. Like Data-X never happened.

Meanwhile, I've withered to a shell of a man, haunted by flashbacks and urges for violence.

Nolan and Denali deserve so much better than what I have to offer.

I sure as hell hope I don't fuck this up.

~

*Agent Dune*

Charlie leans back, eyes crossing from reviewing hours of meaningless video feed. His phone buzzes and he picks it up.

"Agent Gray."

"Dune. I sent you a link. The Mexican lab didn't house any humans. They were doing animal testing there. Wolves."

Ice pours across the surface of his skin.

*Wolves.*

A memory, long buried. His grandfather and uncles pulling down their shotguns to hunt a wolf.

Jesus.

What is he thinking now? There isn't such thing as a wolf-man.

A werewolf.

"I have the name of the funder. Looks like he was a

major funder of Data-X as well. Santiago Rodriguez. Formerly of Lobo Mountain, Mexico. Currently resides in Honduras. Also funds an animal testing lab in Barcelona. It's all in the files I uploaded."

"Thank you." His voice sounds gruff because his mind is stuttering and repeating and stuttering again over the wolf thing. "Gray? Were there animals at any of the Data-X labs?" He clears his voice. "Wolves?"

"That information is all redacted."

*Yeah, but you could probably get into it.*

They both pause, and he knows she hears his unspoken sentence.

"I'll see what I figure out."

"Thanks, Gray. I appreciate it."

"Don't thank me yet."

# 7

# D*enali*

I WAKE up to the sound of the door opening and shutting and heavy footfalls. I stretch, my lioness more than content with having a male in the house.

I didn't really feel right making Nash sleep on the couch, but if he moved straight into my bedroom, Nolan would really think he's here to stay. And that still remains to be determined.

I get out of bed and jump in the shower. My routine since Nolan's birth has been to try to get my shower in before he wakes up and needs me. Of course, there's another adult in the house now if he wakes. Not that Nash would know what to do with Nolan.

Nolan wakes up and comes into the bathroom just as I'm finishing. "Momma?"

"Yes, baby?"

"Nash is still here, and he bought donuts."

"Did he now?" Well, my kid doesn't need the sugar rush, but the thought was nice.

"He said I have to ask you before I can have one."

"You can have one after you drink a cup of milk. Go ask Nash to pour some milk in one of your sippies." I'm hoping Nash can handle that. I guess I'm testing him a little.

When I come out, I find Nash and Nolan sitting at the kitchen table, each with a donut and a cup of milk. They're discussing cars. I don't know whether little boys find locomotion so fascinating because it gets pushed on them, or because there's some innate male attraction to it, but my kid sure has the itch.

"I like articulating tractors," he tells Nash.

Nash wipes the milk from his mouth with the back of his hand and glances at me. "He just said *articulating*."

"I know. Isn't it cute?" I know my grin is goofy, but wings flap in my chest at the simple pleasure of having someone to share our son's adorable brilliance.

"I got you a coffee. Wasn't sure how you take it."

"Thank you. I like cream, no sugar."

Wow. Are we really going to be learning how to make each other's coffee here?

Things just got real.

I pick up the warm paper cup and take a sip. Nash bought a dozen donuts of all different varieties. I pick out my favorite, a bear claw, and sink my teeth into the sweet doughy treat.

"So, ah, what are you doing today?"

His gaze flicks to Nolan, then back to me. "Working."

Ah. A fight.

"What time?"

"Two in the afternoon. I'll drive down to San Diego and make it back here in time to take you to dinner. Okay?"

I chew the bear claw. "Are you asking me out?"

"Can I have another donut?" Nolan interjects.

"No," I say.

"Drink your milk," Nash says.

I hide my smile. We sure sound like a married couple.

"Yeah, I'm asking you out. I want to buy you a nice meal somewhere."

"Both of us?" I ask doubtfully. Nice meals don't work well with three-year-olds.

"Yeah?" He looks unsure. He doesn't have a clue what it's like to entertain a preschooler while waiting for food at a restaurant.

"I'll see if I can get a sitter."

"A sitter. Okay, right. Good idea. I'll be back here by six." He unfolds his long frame from the kitchen table and even though I need him to leave so I can get Nolan and myself out the door on time, I find myself disappointed.

He hesitates, like he wants to kiss me goodbye, but knows better. Instead he lifts his hand. "See you later."

"Later, alligator," Nolan says.

Nash smiles and leaves, his broad shoulders filling the doorframe as he walks through it.

Crazy man.

Sexy, beautiful lion.

∼

*Nash*

. . .

I GET BACK to Temecula in time to hike in the hills behind Denali's house and pick wildflowers. I'm acting like a fucking teenager going on his first date. And honestly? I feel that out of my depth. I don't know the first thing about being Denali's mate or Nolan's dad. But I definitely want to learn.

Mrs. Davenfield watches me through her window as I hike down the hill with the flowers in hand. I'm pretty sure I see her smile, so I figure I'm safe from the shotgun for tonight, at least.

I knock on the door. Denali answers wearing a slinky red wraparound dress. The kind that dips low in the front and shows off every curve of her delectable body. Yeah. I'm definitely going to have a hard time concentrating through dinner.

I hand her the wildflowers and a smile lights up her beautiful face. I don't get a hello kiss or anything, but then, we have an audience.

Nolan's losing his shyness. He runs over and stops next to his mom. I hold out my knuckles and he gives me a fist bump.

A young woman sits on the couch, fiddling with her phone.

"This is Ashley," Denali says. "She's going to babysit Nolan while we go out."

I give her the hairy eyeball, because I don't trust anyone to watch our kid. But then, I know jack about watching a kid, so who am I to judge?

"We won't be long," Denali tells Ashley as she puts the wildflowers in a vase of water.

I place my hand on her lower back as we head out to my car. It's been years since I've had a date. Maybe since high school. But being a gentleman to Denali comes easy to me. I must be channeling my last foster father, a geeky but kind man who modeled perfect manners at all times. I felt like such a fish out of water with them. I know now it was because I was a shifter, I always had that sense I didn't belong. I couldn't understand all the nice people living placid lives.

No wonder I joined the Marines straight out of high school.

I open the door for Denali and wait for her to get in.

"What are you thinking about?" she asks when I climb in my side and start the car.

I laugh. "Truthfully? I was remembering how my last foster father used to hold doors open for his wife. He was a good man." I pull out and head toward a restaurant Laurie picked out for us. He promised it would be romantic.

"What happened to your parents?" Denali asks gently.

I shrug. I haven't told anyone in years. Since high school, probably. "My dad killed my mom." My throat closes on the words and a shudder runs through me.

I'm grateful Denali withholds the usual gasp. She does lay her slender hand on my knee, though. "Were you there?" Denali whispers.

"Yeah. I mean, I think so. I don't remember the actual killing. But I remember her body. Her throat was torn out. I couldn't believe how much blood there was. I know now he must've been the lion. And his animal killed her when he was in a drunken rage."

Denali clutches her stomach.

"I know. It's disgusting."

"I'm just... sorry. I'm sorry you went through that."

"So you were raised by humans?"

I nod. "Yeah. Had no idea I was a shifter until the war. But this isn't date-worthy conversation."

"No, it is." Denali sounds firm. "We don't really know each other yet. We shared a traumatic experience and have a wonderful kid to show for it. But other than favorite cookies and flowers and color, we don't know each other."

"You're right." I pull up at the restaurant and park. Suddenly I feel trapped by our past. I don't know how to ever move past it and into something brighter.

Red flutters on the edges of my vision, and suddenly, I'm back in the bowels of Data-X.

*I'm strapped to the table, head and limbs secured. My gut is on fire. Even if I could move, I'm not sure I want to look.*

*Someone moves around the table. White lab coat. Smyth, Director of Data-X experiments.*

*"Doctor?" an accented voice murmurs just before shoes click on the floor, along with a tap of a cane. I close my eyes at the smell of expensive cologne. "How is our prime subject?"*

*"Better.*

*"Did you ever find the breeder he was so taken with?"*

*"Unfortunately, no." Smyth jabs a needle into my arm with more force than necessary. The sting barely registers in the mass of pain that's my broken body.*

*"Do you want me to have my men find her?"*

*"Do as you will, Santiago. The Alpha Project is my main concern."*

*I grit my teeth—whatever Smyth just pumped me with burns like acid in my blood.*

*"Of course. In your pursuit of the master race, do not forget who your donors are." The voice fades as fresh pain drags me into darkness... My last thought before I lose consciousness: first, kill Smyth. Then Santiago.*

. . .

"Nash? Nash?"

Fuck. "Give me a second."

"You went somewhere for a minute. More than a minute, actually."

"Yeah," I press a thumb and finger into my eyes, trying to get my vision to clear.

"You just had a flashback."

Gritting my teeth, I nod.

"Do you get them often?"

"All the time."

"What can I do?"

"Talk to me. Tell me something."

"Um. Okay. Nolan did art at preschool today. They learned about animals of the jungle. He drew a lion with lightning shooting out of its eyes."

A laugh slices through me, painful at first. My chest eases a little.

"I'm going to get it framed." Denali's voice washes over me, warm as sunshine.

"Denali..." I need to tell her. I'll never be fit to be a part of Nolan's life. "These visions, I'll never be free."

"You want to talk about it?"

I shake my head.

"Maybe you should."

"No. It's not safe. Can't risk my lion taking over."

"He wouldn't hurt me."

"You don't know that. He's a killer."

"Tell me about when he first came out."

"Yeah. It was in Afghanistan, in the middle of a firefight. My unit was pinned down. Watched my friends die around me. And then everything went black."

"He came out to protect you." Denali rests a hand on the

back of my neck. Her touch is enough to relax the taut muscles.

"I thought I was going crazy."

"I'll bet." Denali's fingers swirl over my skin as she muses, "Twenty is late to first see your animal. You must have repressed him a long time. He saw his chance and took it."

"He comes out in the presence of death."

"Or a mate. I met him that night."

"I can't let him out. There's no telling what he'd do." Who he'd kill. All I have to do is remember the sight of my mother's dead body to want to never, ever let my lion out again. Especially with the way my lion thirsts for blood since I got out of Data-X. I squeeze my eyes shut. "He thrives on violence. Bloodshed. That's why I went to Smyth. He said he could rehabilitate me and my lion. He said he'd help."

"Fuck."

"Yeah." I laugh harshly. I can't help myself. "Yeah, that about sums it up." I rub my face with a rough hand. "Come on, let's go in." I open my door and walk around to open hers, but she's already out, her mile-long legs set off by a pair of high heeled strappy sandals.

We go in and are seated. We order a bottle of local wine to share and fresh oysters for an hors d'oeuvre.

Denali's watching me with her long-lashed eyes. Her face is soft, so forgiving. It's hard to imagine I haven't scared her away already with what I've told her.

"I'm fucked up, Denali. It started before Data-X. Way before. I was born this way."

She shakes her head. "That's not true. Our animals aren't bad or wrong. You just think that because you were raised by humans and because of what your dad did."

I shake my head slowly. "My lion is dangerous. And I

feel like these flashbacks—they're from that part of me. If I could get rid of my beast, I would."

Denali's eyes fly wide with horror, and she opens her mouth to speak, then closes it again. She takes a sip of wine, as if to gather her thoughts. "Tell me... in your flashback... what did you see?"

I drain my wine and scrub a hand over my face. "This last one? I was in the lab, with Smyth."

Her hand covers mine on the table. "He can't hurt you. Didn't you say he's dead?"

*Do you want me to have my men find her?* The hairs on my arms raise as I remember the thick accented voice speaking to Smyth. *Santiago.* "Not him. There was another..."

I jump as something buzzes next to us.

"It's okay. It's only my phone." She pulls it out. "Shit, it's the babysitter. I've got to take this."

I nod and drink down my water, trying to squeeze my feelings back into my body. A grown shifter, a lion no less, reduced to panic.

"Um, Denali?" I hear the babysitter's hesitation through the phone.

Denali tenses. "What's wrong?"

"Nothing... Nolan is fine. It's just... a bunch of guys just showed up. We're inside and they're in the driveway."

"White Camaro?" I ask loudly enough for the babysitter to hear.

"Yes. Three guys."

"It's okay," Denali says quickly, "We know them. We'll come right back."

"Okay," the babysitter sounds relieved. "I mean, it's no trouble. They haven't come up to the house, but they're standing around the car and... I think they might be drinking." She pauses and says in a much more admiring tone, "One of them has an Irish accent."

"We'll be right there. Keep Nolan inside," Denali says. As soon as she hangs up, I curse.

"Your pack was serious about their babysitting offer." A smile plays around her lips.

"I'm glad you think this is funny."

"They certainly are trying." She sobers. "We need to lay some ground rules so they can make mischief, but not trouble."

"No need," I growl. "They can't make trouble if they're dead."

I throw some money on the table and we leave without our oysters or dinner.

When we pull up to the house, the white Camaro is still parked in front. Laurie and Parker stand on either side while Declan sits on the hood, a telltale bottle beside him. The Irish man is shirtless, flaunting swirling black tribal tattoos.

As soon as he sees us he launches into song "In the Jungle."

Denali giggles.

I glare at her.

"Oh, come on." Her long legs flex as she steps out of the car. "It is a little funny."

I growl under my breath. Denali heads to the house, where the babysitter and Nolan stand at the door, watching everything unfold with wide eyes.

I stalk to the Camaro.

Declan points to me as he sings "lion."

"Ah-wee-mo-wet, ah-wee-mo-wet," Parker and Laurie chant as Declan takes the high notes, leaning back with arms outstretched until he almost falls off the hood. I grab him and pull him the rest of the way down.

Across the way, Mrs. Davenfield has come out of her house to stand on the porch.

"What the fuck are you doing?" I say through gritted teeth.

"Oh, come on, Alpha—"

"Not your alpha—"

"—we were just havin' a bit o' fun—"

"We thought you were inside." Laurie peers over the hood at us, his glasses magnifying his eyes.

"Yeah, where were you?" Parker asks.

"I was on the date," I grind out and look at Laurie. "Remember? You looked up a restaurant for me."

"Oooooooh," the three chorus.

"I'm guessing we interrupted something good." Parker waggles his grey brows.

"Coitus—" Declan starts, and I push him against the car.

"I. Am. Going. To. Kill—"

"Nash… it's okay," Denali calls. She approaches with the babysitter, who stares at Declan with admiration. Nolan trots along behind.

Shit. I'm about to brawl with my own pack on my mate's front lawn. In front of a three-year-old.

"Baby, stay on the porch," Denali says as she pays the babysitter.

"But, momma, I want to play."

"I got him." Laurie lopes to Nolan. The gawky shifter kneels to speak to the boy.

"We didn't mean to cause trouble," Parker tells Denali. "You could've stayed out on your date."

"We got a call that three strange men were in the driveway," I growl. "What do you think we were going to do?"

"Ya weren't scared o' us, were ya, luv?" Declan turns to the babysitter, taking her hand and kissing it.

"Oh no." She flutters her lashes at him. "I just wasn't sure who you were."

"Declan O'Connor, at your service. Would be pleased to get to know ya better."

The woman beams at Declan as he walks her to her car.

Nolan shouts something to his mom about showing Laurie his trucks, and the two disappear.

"No harm, no foul," Parker murmurs.

I blow out a breath. My lion still wants to kill someone.

"Nash." Denali puts a hand on my back, and some of the tension ebbs away. "It's all right. Really. I like your crazy friends."

Friends. I don't really consider them that, but I suppose they are. The last time I called men friends they all got killed. I guess I haven't chosen to be close to anyone since then.

These goofballs have been worming themselves into my life despite my best efforts to keep them out.

Crazy fucks.

~

*Denali*

When I come out from putting Nolan to sleep, Nash is on the prowl, moving softly around the cottage, looking through windows without moving the shades.

I should be scared to know he truly believes we're in danger. It's hard to feel scared with such a vigilant protector, though.

I have this crazy desire to ease his tension, too. Which is weird, because I'm supposed to be keeping him at a distance. I guess my lioness doesn't understand that part. She sees him as mate. Mine to soothe. To satisfy. To invite to bed.

Aw, shit. I'm totally going to invite him into my bed.

Yeah, him sleeping on the couch only lasted one night. Well, I can't help it. All last night I thought about what it'd be like to have him sleeping beside me. Would he hold me against his chest like he did that night in the cell?

Would sleeping to the sound of his beating heart be as comforting as I imagine it will be?

I walk up beside him and wrap my arms around his waist. "Everything okay?"

"Yeah." He turns and buries a hand in my hair, lifts my face to his. "Sorry we never got dinner."

I smile up at him. "I got what I needed."

"Which is?"

"Time alone with you."

Pain flickers over his face, as if he thinks he fucked up that time. Honestly, knowing he has PTSD isn't a deterrent for me. I think I'd be more worried about him and his character if he didn't. If I'd had any doubts that he was as damaged as I was by Data-X, they're completely gone. He may have joined voluntarily, but he was a tortured prisoner same as I was.

His fear of his lion does cause me some worry, though. You can't repress such a powerful animal. It's probably why his lion needs to fight when he finally lets it out. Or wait—does he fight in lion form?

I make a mental note to check out one of his fights. I need to see what this male does for a living, as sordid as it may be.

Nash leans his forehead against mine and drags a

knuckle down my breastbone until he reaches my cleavage. "This dress is making my pants too tight."

The laugh that comes out of my lips sounds husky. "Oh yeah?"

He pinches one nipple, hard. Like the other times we've had sex, I'm thrilled by his aggression. It's the one place he doesn't hold back with me. I'm always slightly shocked by it, in a way that goes straight to my core. "Yeah."

"Wanna get it off me?"

A low, leonine growl erupts from his throat.

I laugh and turn, taking off running for my bedroom.

It takes him a half-second to follow, the loud slam of his boots ringing on the simple pine planks of the floor. He lets me get all the way to the bedroom before he catches me up by the waist. His mouth is at my neck, teeth grazing my skin.

"Ran from me, did you?" His voice is deep, dark with promise.

Oh God, I hope he wants to punish me again.

"I-is there a consequence for that?" I sound breathless.

He laughs darkly. "Damn straight there is." He makes a big show out of unbuckling his belt and drawing it out of the loops.

I swallow, thinking I've bit off more than I can chew, but he winds it around my wrists, cinching with the buckle and pulling it high over my head. My arms lift like a marionette's.

He tosses the end of the belt over the top of the door and shuts the door, trapping it there. I'm now strung up to the door. "Mmm." He steps back and eyeballs me, approvingly. "Now that's a sight I've been fantasizing about all night." He steps forward and yanks open the sides of my wrap around dress, exposing my white lace bra. "Except more like this."

He pulls back again and gives his cock a squeeze through his pants.

Even though the buckle pokes into my wrist a bit, I let myself stretch and hang from the belt, like I'm trying to escape.

Nash moves in and slams me back against the door, his mouth on mine. "Trying to escape me, my queen?"

"Mmmf," is all I can say, because he claims my mouth again as soon as he speaks. "Beautiful, beautiful lioness."

One of his hands works into my bra as the other grabs my ass. I lift one leg to wrap around his waist, snapping my hips to meet his slow thrusts. He pinches and rolls my nipple, a maddening torture that turns my pussy wet. I sway against the hold of the belt, my knees turning weak. He drags his mouth down my neck at the same time he unties the wrap to my dress, letting it swing open. He has the full view of my white lace bra and panties, which set off my mocha skin. I went out and bought them this afternoon just for our date.

"Fuck, Denali," Nash growls. "Do you have any idea what you do to me?" His eyes glow yellow. Mine have probably turned grey-blue. Nash wraps a fist in my curls and holds my head captive for another savage kiss. As his lips twist over mine, he shoves both cups of my bra down and mauls my breasts. I wrap both legs around his waist and he bites my lower lip, holding it between his teeth and pulling. "I'm gonna fuck you right up against this door, Denali. And you'd better hold your screams in, because if you wake up the boy, I'm not going to let you come."

"*Let* me come?" I let out an indignant laugh.

He rips the seam on the side of my new panties and yanks them off me. "You heard me." There's challenge in his voice, which I love.

I use my legs around his back to yank him closer, rubbing my bare pussy over the crotch of his jeans.

He lets out a harsh curse and unbuttons them. His cock springs out, large and glorious. I'm grateful he has the presence of mind to produce a condom, because the thought hadn't even crossed my mind. He rolls it on and slams into me with one brutal thrust.

My entire back presses against the door. I'm suspended by Nash's body, my pelvis lifted by his, which gives my wrists relief.

Nash bites my neck, pulling back and slamming in again. "I have you exactly the way I want you, baby."

"Yes," I gasp. He fills me, satisfying me in the way I never knew I needed. Each thrust is a pact, a promise. He needs me. I need him. The mating bond is unbreakable. Our animals have chosen. "God, yes."

Nash holds my thighs and drills into me, rattling the door on its hinges with each thump, thump, thump of our bodies slamming against it.

We move as one, in perfect communion, perfect rhythm. I yield to his claiming as I yielded that first night and suddenly it becomes clear.

I wasn't forced.

Data-X may have demanded we breed, but our animals chose each other, regardless. Nash mate-marked me because we're mates, not because he lost control under duress. In fact, Data-X did us a favor by helping us find each other.

I nearly weep with the significance of my discovery just as Nash starts to lose control. His movements grow jerky, thighs shaking as he plows into me.

"You ready to come, baby?"

"You going to let me?" I purr.

He loses it. His thrusts become frantic. "Fuck, yeah. Come, for me, beautiful lioness."

I surrender completely, let him fill and empty me, sawing in and out until my desire passes the breaking point.

I yank my wrists against the belt, squeeze my thighs around his waist, yanking him deeper. He swallows my scream with a kiss and we both come to a simultaneous finish, my pussy squeezing around his pulsing cock.

"You're mine," I chant. "You're mine, you're mine."

Nash lets out a shaky laugh and cups my face. "Am I?" He hooks his forearm under my ass to lift me and releases the belt from over the door. I pull my wrists out as he carries me to the bed. He lays me down and kisses the red marks on my skin where the belt dug in.

"You really gonna claim me, baby?" Nash rumbles.

"Yes." I reach for him and run my fingers through his hair. I mean it, too. Nash is my mate. Our animals have chosen. The rest, we'll figure out.

# 8

D*enali*

THE PIT IS on the wasted edge of an industrial area. I park my beat-up car near the edge of a lot filled with trucks and motorcycles. The air is heavy with the smell of animals. One tang slips through—Nash's scent. I draw in a deep breath and march to the door, striding in leather ankle boots and a black miniskirt that shows off the length of my legs. A black tube top hugs my torso. Kohl around my eyes and thin gold hoops in my ears, my hair in a soft 'fro, and my natural scent screams what I am: a lioness on the prowl.

I get plenty of pointed looks from a few tatted dudes smoking joints by their bikes. More shifters turn as I enter the dark building. A few wolves lounge by the door, leather cuts marking them as the "Timberland pack." They're a motley crew of mohawks and bad tattoos. They straighten as I pass, hooting in my direction. I give them a look and bare my teeth. Their eyes light up shifter bright before they all duck their heads and turn away from my more dominant animal.

My lioness smirks a little. They must not be used to lady cats here. Wrinkling my nose at the stench of beer and urine, I understand why. I prefer classier bars.

I get as far as the bar before I hesitate. I know there's a fight here somewhere, but I don't want to ask.

A tall man launches himself from the corner. "Denali." Laurie blinks at me from behind his Coke bottle glasses. "You're here. Does Nash—"

"No. I wanted to come. I wanted to see." If Nash is going to be in my life, in Nolan's life, I want to know everything about him. Good, bad, and ugly.

Besides, I've always wanted to see a fight.

His Adam's apple bobs as he swallows. "Are you sure—"

"I'm sure," I infuse my voice with dominance. "Take me to him, Laurie."

The smell of animals grows thicker as we descend a long staircase, a miasma of fur and blood. My lioness pushes to the fore, until the gloom lifts under my own eyes' light. I realize the noise I've been hearing is a dull roar coming from the seething sea of shifters. The floor seems to move, the boom of voices gives this place its own heartbeat.

"Full house tonight." I lick my lips. My skin buzzes, my heart pounds from proximity to so many other shifters. My lioness is excited, straining to take it all in. I feel… alive.

"It's always full when Nash fights." Laurie points to the center of the room, and I catch my breath. A huge, scar-faced shifter stands bare-chested in the middle of a fighting cage. His head and shoulders are so big he looks like he has no neck. He beats his chest and roars. The shouting crowd echoes his violent lust, beating on the metal links as the challenging fighter slips into the ring. The newcomer has a crew cut and an American flag on his shoulders.

Nash.

My foot wobbles on the stair. Nash surveys the crowd with blind eyes, ignoring his growling opponent. At one point, his head snaps toward the stairs. I duck, slinking behind some cheetahs with MC patches, willing my cat scent to blend with theirs. When I glance back up, Nash has turned away to talk to Parker. Their heads bend toward each other as they confer a moment, then Nash shrugs the flag off and folds it carefully, handing it to the smaller shifter. Parker slips out quickly and closes the door. His voice comes over the loudspeaker a second later, announcing the start of the fight. Boos and cheers drown him out.

"Who's he fighting?" I ask Laurie. The beanstalk shifter leans close.

"Bear. Down from Alaska. They call him *Grizz*."

"He's huge. Don't they do weigh-ins on fighters?"

"Not these fights." Laurie's laugh huffs past my ears, his feathery scent tickles my nose. "Just watch."

The bell clangs and the two animals start circling each other. The grizzly is surprisingly light on his feet. Nash's face holds a look of concentration. A few light punches start the action, and the scar-faced shifter wades in, slamming a haymaker at Nash's head. Nash dodges gracefully out of the way, and the crowd murmurs. They want a good fight. They want to see blood.

The grizzly goes nuts, head down, shoulders hunched. His fists are a machine, throwing heavy punches in a constant, deadly rhythm. Nash gets in a few hits but mostly he dances, weaving this way and that. The bruin bellows in frustration and comes faster. His arms blur. I clutch at Laurie.

"Just watch," he repeats.

Nash toys with the grizzly, turning lightly on his feet. A game, a dance, and the crowd grows restless. They start cheering the bear, who comes and comes and comes.

"He's wearing him out," I breathe, just as the grizzly's fist catches Nash's shoulder. Nash's arm snaps back, retaliating with a brutal punch to the fighter's already scarred face. I hear the crunch from across the room. Blood sprays. The crowd groans in pleasure, the fur scent growing. Around us hands sprout claws and canines lengthen. Nash keeps moving, light and fluid.

My lioness scratches to the surface, unbelievably turned on by seeing Nash's prowess in the cage.

"King of the Beasts," the crowd chants. Shifters press against the cage, fingers reaching through the links in an attempt to touch their liege. They love him. They want him, the beautiful violence he gives. He embodies their beasts, their need. The blood he spills satisfies them more than sex, and they crave more and more.

They can't have him. He's mine.

Before I know it, I'm pushing through the crowd, all the way up to the cage. A wolf growls as I push past him. One glance at my lioness' eyes and he whimpers, ducking his head. If he had a tail in human form, he'd tuck it between his legs.

*King of the Beasts*, they call Nash. And every king needs a queen.

I take my place at the front. Nothing separates me from the fighters but a flimsy bit of metal. It smells slightly of silver—some sort of alloy to keep shifters off, probably. I grip the links and relish the slight burn. And wait.

Nash's head snaps in my direction. I smile. His eyes widen, pupils lighting to pure blazing amber.

*Hey baby,* my lioness purrs. He shakes his head as if he can't believe I'm really here.

He mouths my name, and I practically feel his breath on my skin.

"Who's the bitch?" the grizzly chuffs, and Nash's eyes light up gold. The bruin doesn't see it, still mocking me. He doesn't have a chance.

Nash whirls, and bowls into the grizzly's thick chest. There's no more art, just wild blows that fall with deadly force. The grizzly tries to counter, but each punch drives him back, sends him reeling so his return hits go wide. Finally, the grizzly crumples. Nash slams him to the ground, roaring his victory. I feel the sound in every part of my body. The crowd surges behind me.

Parker opens the door and shifters rush the cage, pushing inside. He cranes his neck, looking for me through the crowd chanting— "King, king, king."

"Like the fight?" Declan says at my side.

"Where is he?" I half snarl with need.

Declan's mouth tugs up in a grin. "I'll take you to him."

But crossing the room takes forever. Declan finally leads me to the wall, where we slide past a crazed shifter, howling at nothing, strung out and high from the energy of the fight. At last we reach the far side and a private door. "Through there." Declan holds it for me. "Down the hall. Turn right when you see the lockers. You can follow the scent of blood."

Heart pounding in my ears, I stride down the hall. The walls pulse with the roar of the crowd. But I catch a whiff of a spice-laden scent.

"Nash," I whisper, and hurry along.

He's alone in the locker room, blood streaking his back,

his head bent as he leans against the lockers. A warrior, beaten but not broken. My warrior.

"Nash," I breathe.

He turns, and I rush him, leaping at the last second. He catches me easily, hands cupping my ass as I literally jump him.

I slam my mouth down on his.

∽

*Denali*

*In Nash's arms I forget the cell, the guards. I forget everything but the pull of his lips on mine.*

*I'm a new creation, all hot desire and electric sensation. My heartbeat trips as Nash breaks the kiss and fastens his mouth to my neck, teeth scraping over my pulse.*

*I whimper, hips jerking against him. He's solid and strong, body taut and impressive. I wrap my legs around his waist and he lifts me, maneuvering me back on the bed so I'm under him, safe and protected.*

*"Denali," he growls, eyes glowing amber. I'm sure mine are grey-blue. "I'm losing control. You should stop me—"*

*"I don't want to stop." I've never been with another lion before. I had no idea how compelling his closeness could be. I yank him closer. I can't get enough of his scent, his heat, his hips cradled in mine. He's trying to be considerate but it's only pissing me off. "Stop holding back," I growl. "Give it to me, Nash. I want this." Lifting my pelvis, I rub my wet center against his hard length.*

*He drives into me with a force that steals my breath. The cot creaks and groans under the force of his thrusts. Somewhere outside, I think I hear the guards cheering us on. I couldn't care less. Nothing matters but the incredible sensation of Nash moving inside me. He's just spent thirty minutes with his mouth glued to my center, licking me to orgasm after orgasm, but it wasn't enough.*

*This is what I needed.*

*He braces his arms against the wall above my head to drive even deeper, harder.*

*I should've known what was coming.*

*Sharp fangs lengthened in his mouth. But all I could think was more. Now. Yes. All I knew was the intense pleasure of him filling me. Claiming me.*

*My head hits the concrete wall and I reach up to brace myself, but Nash curses and pulls out. In a flash, I'm on my knees facing the wall, hands splayed on the smooth grey surface and he's entering me from behind. I arch back for him, pushing my ass out and he grips my hips with a bruising force.*

*He slams into me over and over again until I lose my mind completely. Stars spark behind my eyes. I hear a snarl, but I don't know whether it came from me or him. The roar was him—it's a fucking lion's roar and I have no doubt every human or shifter in the place heard it. Probably every creature for five square miles heard it and took cover. There's no mistaking a lion's roar.*

*Nash shoves deep and stays. I shudder and clench around him as my mind orbits the moon. I don't come back to my body until Nash's teeth snap onto my shoulder.*

*Pain sears but it's quickly followed by euphoria. My lioness roars back.*

*Nash marked me.*

*I should be pissed. I should turn around and slap his face. But all I feel is bliss.*

*My body shakes and trembles as I tumble around on a high I've never known before.*

*Nash pulls me to sit on his lap and licks the wound closed. "Denali. Fuck. Denali. Talk to me. Are you okay? I'm so sorry. I didn't mean for that to happen."*

*My eyelids drift to half-mast and I cover his mouth to shut him up. My purr is my only answer.*

∾

NASH

SHE'S all mating scent and greedy hands roving over my sweat slicked body.

"You came. You watched the fight."

"Yes." She rocks against me. "Yes. I have to have you."

Even with her mouth against mine, my thoughts stray. She saw me at my worst, most violent, my animal out and wild.

"Denali, please—"

"I need you," she pants. "I need you."

I stop trying to make sense of it. I hitch up her skirt and suck in a breath. She's not wearing panties. Fuck, she's not wearing anything but a tiny strip of fabric over her breasts and another one around her hips. Her skin is warm and smooth and clean, and I could die happy. Maybe I did. Maybe I died in the cell and now I'm in heaven.

"King of the beasts." She nuzzles me, like a cat begging to be stroked.

"Only if you're my queen," I growl and back her against the lockers. I shove down my pants and free my erection, fumbling in my bag for the condom in my wallet. She purrs as she helps me roll it on and guides me to her entrance.

It's so wrong. I shouldn't fuck my mate in this nasty

place, but she wants it and I'm incapable of denying her. I surge into her.

Her head flies back, fingernails digging into my back. "Mine," her lioness growls, ripping at my back with her nails every time I thrust.

"Yes." I kiss her, embracing the pain, loving the feel of her claim. Why she would *want* to lay claim to me is bewildering after what I just did up there, but I'll take what I can get. This female is the only one I've ever cared about. The one I couldn't forget. Couldn't let go.

Well now I've found her, and she wants me back. It seems unbelievable.

I hold one of her thighs up, draped over my arm, which is braced against the wall. I have a good angle to drill into her and I use enough force to bend the metal lockers behind her.

"Denali," I rasp.

"Claim me, lion," she dares.

I laugh. Fuck, it's the first time I've laughed in years. It's not that anything's funny, it's this incredible lightness stealing over me. Denali wants me. She's not afraid. She *likes* my aggression.

I thrust harder and harder, the steam behind my orgasm gathering into a storm of passion. I'm nearly mindless with lust, finding focus is a struggle but I reach around and work a finger between her buttcheeks.

She cries out the moment I find her anus. Her face contorts, mouth opening. Her pussy squeezes tight around my cock, pulsing as she jerks and flails with her orgasm.

I roar as loud as I did that night I marked her. Loud enough to shake the walls. The blood beats in my ears as I slam into her once, twice, five more times and then I'm coming.

The room spins, sweat drips into my eyes.

She giggles into my neck. "The whole building went silent after you roared. Bet they didn't know how loud a lion can be when he's claiming his mate."

I'm glad she thinks it's funny, because I suddenly feel like a first-class asshole. Does everyone in The Pit know I just claimed her?

As soon as I let her feet touch the ground, she sags against me. I touch her dark skin, smooth as polished walnut, and rub it like a talisman. But when I take my hand away, my fingers are smeared with rust. I grip her shoulders. "Fuck."

"Nash?"

"Blood... on your body..." My breath saws from my lungs. My hands flutter over her, my vision narrowing. Oh God. I always knew I'd hurt her. I'm not fucking safe.

"It's okay. Baby, it's okay. It's not mine. You're covered in it."

Oh. Right. The fight. Thank fuck.

"I'm sorry." I sag in relief. The gore on her skin—it's straight from my nightmares.

"It's okay. Let me," she tugs me toward the showers and turns on the water. Holding the detachable shower head, she rinses the gore from my skin, massaging with her free hand until I close my eyes.

The skin is already healed, healthy. I haven't healed this quickly in... I don't know how long.

"Better?" she asks, handing me a towel.

I dry off, then reach for her. My arms close around her slender form. She's all sinuous power packed into a delicate feminine package. "Denali," I drop my head to her marked shoulder, breathing in our mingled scents. She's warm and smooth. Her arms feel like home.

"Come on, baby. Let me take you home."

∼

*Nash*

"*Favorite movie?*"

"*Lion King,*" *I say, and Denali snorts. We're lying in each other's arms. Her hands roam up and down my back, tracing the planes and grooves of my muscles. "What about you?"*

*Her gaze darts away. She blinks, her eyes growing misty. "Born Free."*

*I tighten my hold on her. "Denali, I'm going to get you out—"*

*The door slams open. I jerk upright, claws out, but they're ready for me. The shock sticks hit my body. My knees give out, but the pain is nothing compared to the screams of my mate as they drag her away from me.*

# 9

## Denali

HE STALKS me through the pine trees. I can't hear the tread of his heavy paws, but I know he lopes just behind. The moment I pulled up in the parking area at the base of the Temescal Ridge trail, I yanked off my clothes and shifted, leaving Nash sputtering in bewilderment.

*Catch me, lion.*

I want Nash to embrace his animal like I do. He's been making it the enemy for far too long. He should feel the joy of the hunt. Of the chase. Of stretching his long, sleek body out for a fifty mile an hour run.

I left Nolan at preschool and rearranged my appointments. I could've brought Nolan with us, but Nash is so unsure of his lion. I need to give him my full attention and I don't want him worrying about fathering Nolan. Because even though he's cautiously attempting the role, I know he's still getting used to it.

I love letting my lioness out. Running at top speeds, chasing rabbits, tracking scents. I love being wild, one with nature.

A huge paw comes down on my hind end and we tumble to the ground. I roll and spring back up. In a flash I'm down again, on my back. Nash steps on my throat to hold me down, then licks my face. He's magnificent. Bigger than any lion I've ever seen—twice as big as my lioness. His mane is sandy blond, eyes amber. His paws are the size of a dinner plate. His long tail flicks behind him.

Both of us purr. He's happy. I swear I can sense the joy bubbling up in his lion as plainly as I feel the sun on my fur. The dull static I sensed from his animal when I first met him is gone.

He removes the paw holding me down and I scramble up and tussle with him, trying to bring him down. Of course, it's impossible. He toys with me, lets me scamper around him and nip at his throat before he tackles me to the ground again.

Suddenly we're in human form, though I don't remember thinking I wanted to shift. Did his lion somehow alpha command it? Just like the afternoon he showed up at my cottage, I'm on my back beneath him, only this time, we're naked. The forest floor beneath me is soft and springy with undergrowth, nature's gentle bed for two lions.

He rocks his hard erection between my legs. "You like to be chased, my lovely lioness?" He nuzzles my neck.

The head of his cock prods my entrance without guidance from either of us. We don't have condoms with us and I don't think Nash even remembers, but in that moment, I surrender to fate. If we're meant to produce another perfect cub, I'd take it. Everything feels easy and possible with Nash's heart beating over mine.

He thrusts into me leaning up on his hands to keep his weight off. "I love you, Denali."

We both freeze. He has a deer in headlights look, as if he had no idea he was going to say that.

Hard determination slams down on his face. "It's true," he says fiercely. "I don't care if we don't have the longevity to prove we can make it. You're mine."

I lift my hips to urge him to move inside me again. "Is it love or is it a lion's claim?" I ask softly. Because there's a difference. The lion's claim is his animal's choice. Love is a human emotion. Does Nash even know love?

Torment flickers over Nash's face. I see his doubts about himself, what he's become, but he shakes his head. "I wouldn't have said it if it weren't true."

Tears prick my eyes because I believe him. The words had just fallen out. He loves me.

I wrap my arms around his neck. "I love you, too, Nash. You're mine."

His eyes blaze with light and he slams into me. The birds in the trees twitter and chatter, like our energy feeds them. The sky starts swirling above us, or maybe I've grown dizzy with lust. All I know is that everything on the mountain seems to contribute to our mating—the trees, the leaves, the flowers, the other animals. There's a magic in our joining. A beautiful consummation, as if this is our true mating. The one we were destined for. Not that crazed bite back in a cell.

I'm not surprised at all when Nash bellows and sinks his teeth into my shoulder, in the same place he chose last time.

I buck against him, my orgasm unravelling in waves of pleasure and release. There's no pain. Only fulfillment. This was meant to be. A union of shifter souls. We belong together, to each other. There's no denying or escaping it now.

It is done.

~

N*ASH*

I DON'T MEAN to bite Denali. Like the first time, I didn't know I was going to do it until my teeth are already buried in her flesh and I taste her blood. I release her and lick away the blood. "I'm sorry, baby."

"*No.*" She stops me. It's a queen's command. There's no room to argue with her. "This is how we were meant to mate."

Her words sweep through me like a warm breeze. My eyes and nose burn for a moment with the magnitude of it. She's accepted me as her mate.

That scratchy voice in my head that tells me I can't really have her—that I have nothing to offer but my pain and misery and violence—starts up, but I shove him back. I won't let anything take away this moment. It may be the first time in my life I've experienced true happiness. True, full, unadulterated joy.

Denali is mine. The sun is shining, and the birds are chirping. I'm out in nature and no one's trying to kill us. At least at the moment. And my body feels incredible.

It's buzzing with an energy I've never known. Strength and vitality flow through my veins. It's like I've just drunk some elixir that gives me superpowers. Is it from mating with Denali? Or letting my lion run? Or both?

Suddenly, I'm playful again. I roll off Denali and lift her

to her feet. "Then you'd better run, or I'll be showing you all the things my lion wants to do to assert his claim." I slap her ass and shift.

She's off in a flash, the fluffed tip of her tail swishing as she bounds over boulders, her sleek body leaping with boneless grace.

We run for hours, up and down the side of the mountain. A couple hikers come along, and we have to slip into an opening in a rock wall to watch them pass. Then we bound down to a stream where we drink. I haven't been my lion this long before. It's both freeing and terrifying.

What if he grows too strong? What if he doesn't let me shift back? What if he demands to be let out on a regular basis? And my worst fear of all—what if he kills or maims someone?

But I don't feel the dark violence simmering in me the way it usually fuels my gut. The sick lion who has to fight to live seems very far removed from the powerful beast strutting through the forest now. I truly feel like the king of the jungle.

I have no sense of time, but Denali must have better integration of her human senses with her lioness, because she leads me back to the car by early afternoon.

She shifts at the door, then reaches for the handle. It's locked, and I see panic flare in her eyes, because she left the keys on the seat when we arrived.

I shift into human form. "I have them," I tell her, my voice gruff after being in lion form. I grab them from the crook of a tree where I'd hidden them before following her this morning.

Her smile dazzles. "Always looking out for me, aren't you?"

I nod, suddenly dead serious. "Believe it."

She catches my tone and lifts her head, locking gazes with me over the top of the car. She's unabashed about her nudity, which makes it even more spectacular as the afternoon sun makes her skin glow. "I do." Her voice is soft.

Something's changed between us. Something wonderful and serious. The defenses we had up are crumbling and we're on the same side now. A team.

I toss the keys to her and she catches them easily and opens the door. We both pull on our clothes and climb into her little car.

"So, Nash?" Denali slips a sideways glance at me from under her long lashes. Lovely lioness.

"Yeah?"

"How are you feeling about fatherhood?"

Oh God. My heart starts beating faster. This is important. She's asking me something important because of what changed between us today. I need to answer this right.

But I can't lie, either.

"I'm scared shitless," I admit.

She gives a surprised bark of laughter. "I know the feeling. Fates, when Nolan was born I had dreams that the back door of the car had opened up while I was driving, and his car seat was falling out."

"Oh, Christ."

"And I had one where I was still in high school and I'd accidentally left his carrier outside the classroom. Some other kids had picked him up and I was in a panic trying to find him."

I give a rueful laugh. "It's a daunting task. One nobody wants to fuck up."

"Exactly." She looks over again, her gaze sharp. "Are you up for it?"

The back of my neck prickles. Again, I have the sense my response could change the course of my life. Of *our* lives.

"Yeah." I sound wheezy.

"You sure? Because there's no half-assing this. You're either in or you're out. And you don't get me without being all in with Nolan."

The prickles are everywhere now—coursing down my shoulders and spine, along my legs. "I know," my voice sounds strangled. "I'm in. I'm all in, Denali. You're my family."

If it's true, why am I sweating? Why is my heart thundering faster than it did when I ran fifty miles on that mountain?

Do I just *want* it to be true, but I really know I can't?

Or will I be able to prove myself to Denali and Nolan? Become something I never knew I could?

I don't fucking know, but I'd better figure my shit out quick.

# 10

## Nash

I FINISH SCREWING the new security screen door into the door frame at Denali's. I haven't had a fight scheduled for a few days so I've been spending my time fixing things at the cottage. Making sure her place is adequately protected was my first order of business, but I've also repainted her kitchen cabinets and installed a drip watering system for the flowerbeds. I even made friends with Mrs. Davenfield, Denali's nosy landlady, by installing drip in her flowerbeds, too.

Tinkering around like this makes me think maybe I could find a new career—something tamer than fighting or war. Handyman stuff suits me. It's solitary work, but useful. It requires physical strength, which I have, and an ability to problem-solve. Turns out, when my lion isn't clawing to get free, my clear-headedness returns to me.

All this time I was terrified to let my lion out, to shift into lion form. I thought he'd go on a rampage and kill because that's what happened the other times he came out.

Maybe he's just been going crazy because I was suppressing him. That and staying away from my marked mate.

My phone rings and I pull it out and glance at the caller. It's Denali.

"Hey baby. What's going on?"

"Nash, the preschool just called. Nolan's throwing up. I'm totally tied up with my client—I'm in the middle of giving her a bath and I can't leave. Can you go get him?"

I try to muffle my choke of surprise. "Uh, yeah. Will they let me get him?"

"I just sent over my signed permission. You'll have to show ID, but yeah. I told them his father was getting him."

I swallow hard.

*His father.*

Right.

That's me.

Well, shit.

I've been sent on high-stake missions for my country. I've survived torture at the hands of my government. I can totally handle a puking preschooler.

Right?

I get in my car and fumble with the keys. I can do this. I can totally do this. I repeat the mantra the entire ride to the preschool. Then I have to give myself a pep talk to get out of the car.

The doors to the preschool are locked so I have to use a buzzer to be let in. The director comes out to meet me. She definitely gives me the stink eye and a thorough up and down sweep of her eyes. I guess absentee dads don't rate so high here.

I should've been prepared for that.

She leads me to the butterfly room where I find Nolan, lying on a mat in the corner while the other children play. He definitely looks green around the gills.

"Hey, buddy," I say softly.

He climbs to his feet. "Where's momma?"

"She's working. I'm going to take you home."

Nolan starts crying. "I want my momma."

Damn. I have no idea what to do now. Do I pick him up and get the hell out? Try to talk him into coming nicely?

"I know you don't feel good, buddy. I'm going to take care of you. Come here, little man." I'm relieved when he lets me pick him up without a fuss.

His teacher gives me the same suspicious regard as the director, but she helps me out by gathering Nolan's things and showing me how and where to sign him out.

I'm worse than Schwarzenegger in Kindergarten Cop the way I bumble around trying to hold Nolan's lunch and soiled clothing bag and Nolan while I open doors and find my way out.

When we get to my car, I make the stupidest mistake of opening the front side passenger door for him. Instead of climbing in, he stares into the backseat and then wails, "Where's my car seat?"

*Shit!* Car seat... I should know these things. Why didn't Denali say something? And then I remember she'd said something about coming to her work, but I thought she meant I should do that if I couldn't handle it on my own. She was probably telling me to go there first to get the car seat.

Nolan's totally melting down now, hanging from the door handle and bawling.

I don't blame the kid. He's sick and he wants his mom. I'm definitely a far cry from momma. But I'm not about to take him back into the school because I don't have a car seat. I have gotten people through far more dangerous situations than driving a couple miles without a car seat. We'll make it home.

"I'm really sorry, buddy. I don't have the car seat, but I'm going to buckle you up tight in the back seat and I'll have you home in no time, okay?"

No response because he's crying too hard.

This totally sucks.

I open the back door and lift him in, carefully arranging the seat belt around his waist and behind his back so it doesn't choke him. "I'll get you right home, little man."

He throws up all over the back seat just as we arrive at Denali's. I don't really care about anything but the fact that the poor little guy is suffering, though. I pull him out and carry him in, taking him straight to the bathroom to get cleaned up.

I fill the bathtub and strip off his pukey clothes. He calms down in the warm water, although his listlessness worries me even more than the crying. I use a washcloth to clean off his face and offer him his toothbrush to clean the bad taste from his mouth.

I dial Denali while he sits in the tub and stares at the wall. Dark circles loop under his eyes.

"How's he doing?" Denali answers.

"He's pretty sick. Should I give him anything?"

"You mean like medicine? Does he have a fever?"

I touch his head with the back of my hand. "I don't think so."

"Then just whatever he can keep down. Push fluids. Maybe toast. Or applesauce. You know the drill."

I totally don't know the drill, and I feel like an asshole because of it. How many times in Nolan's short life has Denali already had to deal with this sort of thing?

Nolan stands up in the tub.

"Okay, looks like he needs me, I gotta go," I say to Denali.

"Nash?" she says as I'm about to hang up.

"Yeah?"

"You got this, Dad."

*Dad.* I feel pretty fucking far from a dad. The word makes the space between my ribs tighten and I have to force my breath out.

"I'll do my best," I say.

I pull the plug in the tub and wrap a towel around Nolan after I lift him out. He shivers, standing docile and subdued. I dry him quickly and carry him to his room. "Where are your pajamas, bud?"

He points to a drawer and I pull out a pair of Spiderman jammies and make a spectacle out of myself trying to figure out how to dress him.

"I'm going to get you settled on the couch. We'll find a good show for you on television, okay? Do you want anything to eat or drink?"

He shakes his head, so I get him settled and find Curious George on the television.

"Is it okay if I go clean out the car, bud? I'll be right outside if you need me."

Nolan nods so I head outside with a bucket of water and a scrub brush. The whole time I'm out there, I'm worrying about getting inside, getting back to the poor kid, in case he gets sick again or needs me.

Fuck.

If this is what it's like to be a parent, I don't know if I have the emotional stamina for it.

And that's seriously crazy coming from a guy who a month ago was completely emotionally dead.

∽

*Denali*

I COME HOME to find Nolan curled up and sleeping on top of Nash's large body on the couch. Nash has an arm curved around Nolan's soft form, cradling him close.

*Heart. Melted.*

Nash is watching cartoons, which is hilarious and sweet. I'm guessing he didn't want to move to turn off the TV or change the station.

It nearly killed me not to go racing to the preschool myself when they called, but I couldn't get away from my client—especially after I'd rescheduled with her earlier in the week. Plus, I wanted Nash to have a chance to be a dad. I can tell he's majorly uncomfortable with the role. Hell, I was terrified to be a parent, too. But you don't get special training. It's a sink or swim kinda thing and the only way to figure it out is to jump right in. So yeah, taking care of a sick kid is sort of the Parenting 101 crash course.

"How is he?" I murmur, walking over to feel Nolan's forehead. It's clammy, but not hot.

Nash rubs Nolan's cheek with his thumb. "Okay," he whispers. "He's been sleeping for about an hour."

"Thanks for picking him up."

Nash gives an impatient jerk of his head. "Don't thank

me. It's what I should've been doing for the past three years."

I hate how much blame he puts on himself. I touch his shoulder. "And you would have, if I'd let you know about him." I wait until he meets my eye and then a moment longer until he relaxes and nods his agreement.

"Want me to put him in his bed?" I ask.

Nash shakes his head. "No. I've got him."

I smile, and Nash gives a sheepish grin. "I'm pretty proud of myself for getting this far with him."

I run my fingers through his close-cropped hair, massaging his scalp. "As you should be, Daddy."

He only stiffens for a moment at the word *daddy,* which I take as an excellent sign. Nash is finally getting used to his new role.

For the first time in years I'm filled with genuine hope. Maybe Data-X didn't completely fuck up my life forever. Maybe good things are still possible. A loving father for my son. A partner and mate. Maybe even a white picket fence.

This calls for a celebration. I walk to the kitchen and start to hum, taking out the ingredients to make peanut butter cookies.

∼

AGENT DUNE

HE DRIVES by a little cottage sitting on a property with a larger house in Temecula. Nash, the one who set his whole investigation into motion, has been staying here. There's nowhere to stop and set up surveillance because the area is too sparsely populated, so he drives on, not turning around for another mile.

He's been watching the San Diego fighters every minute he can get away. He doesn't know what he thinks he'll see—one of them suddenly sprout hair and drop to all fours? Or go on a jog with a pet wolf?

All he knows is the queasy feeling he's had ever since Gray mentioned *wolves* is only getting stronger.

The Data-X labs were out in the country. He'd assumed it was to keep away from prying eyes, but what if it was because they needed wilderness around for animals?

But was he seriously believing there might be such thing as werewolves?

He remembers the way Nash's eyes glowed yellow. How Charlie picked him up naked, covered in blood after the massacre in Afghanistan. All their men had been shot except Nash. All the insurgents were dead—torn open, body parts scattered as if mauled by a wild animal.

Is Nash a werewolf?

Is Charlie's father?

How did Jared Johnson know? As far as Charlie knows, his own eyes never change color. He never sprouts a tail and howls at the moon.

His father used to show up for a couple days every month, always at night, like seeing them was a big secret. Christ, had it been with the moon?

He gives his head a hard shake. None of this makes sense.

# 11

## Denali

I JERK awake at Nash's cry. He thrashes beside me like he's being electrocuted. In the few weeks since he moved in, I've noticed he twitches with flashbacks or bad dreams at night, but this time is severe. The last time I saw his body jump and convulse like when we were in our cell, as the guards took me away.

"Nash," I breathe, then speak louder. "Nash. It's okay. You're safe."

A scent hits me—cleaning fluid they used to scour the cinder-block walls, washing away the blood. Shifter blood.

"No," I whisper, chills running up and down my arms. This isn't a nightmare. Nash is back in that place, trapped in the memory.

Am I really smelling that place? How? It's like Nash's

flashback seeps into me, too. Must be some kind of mate ability.

I shake Nash's bulging biceps, but I speak to the flashback. "No. You can't have him. He's mine."

With a choked sound, Nash's eyes fly open. "Denali?"

I throw my arms around him. "It's all right. I'm here. Come back to me, baby."

"Denali," he rasps, his hands running over my body. "Denali."

"It's okay," I whisper, holding him close. His huge body shakes and rage surges through me. I wish some of the people from Data-X survived the explosion so I can kill them all over again.

A sound breaks from his throat, not a whimper or sob, but something torn from his body. I hold him tighter. "I'm here, baby. It's me. Your mate. I'm not going to let you go."

"Let her go," he growls, eyes jerking beneath parted lids. He grabs my shoulders roughly and pushes me away. "No," he mumbles. "No. Don't touch her."

"What—"

"No!" Nash roars. He's still in the flashback. His arms fly wide and he catches my face with the back of his hand. I fly off the bed and hit the floor.

A warning snarl comes from my throat, my lioness clawing to the surface to fight, even though Nash isn't the enemy.

"Denali!" Nash bolts out of the bed and stares down at me. His eyes are focused now, hyper alert, and I watch as understanding dawns and horror swims over his face. The light from the little nightlight in the outlet backlights him, making him seem even larger and more dangerous, his clenched fists ready to pummel the enemy.

Except the enemy isn't here.

"Nash?" I stand, rubbing my throbbing cheekbone and approach him carefully, scenting the air. The antiseptic smell of the Data-X prison lab is gone, washed away in the clean night time breeze. "Are you with me?"

"Fuck." It's a broken syllable. He falls to his knees. "*Denali.* Please say I didn't hit you."

I roll my lips together, trying to think of what to say.

He drops his head into his hands. "Oh God. I'm so fucking sorry. This is unforgivable. Unforgivable."

"You were having a flashback," I say. "What was it? Was it about me?"

He lifts his face and beams a haunted gaze at me. "They were going to rape you. I had to stop them. Instead *I* hurt you." His voice breaks.

I sense the static from his lion that I'd felt when he first showed up. The buzzing of a ticking time bomb. An animal about to go berserk.

"I'm okay, Nash. I'm a shifter. I'll heal soon." I want more than anything for him to pull me into his arms, or let me hold him, but he doesn't seem to want to touch me.

He gets up and stumbles back, toward the bedroom door. On the way, he shakes his head and grunts something.

A cold prickle of warning runs through me.

"What?" I make my way to his side until he repeats, "I can't do this."

I halt, dread rising in my throat. "Can't do what?"

"Be here. Be with you and Nolan. I'm too dangerous."

"You can't just leave. Your lion—"

"I'll live. Or I won't. Either way, it's not your problem anymore."

The bedclothes have fallen to the floor. I pick up the sheet and grip it hard. "It *is* my problem." I can't keep my voice level anymore. "It became my problem when you mate-marked me. When you put a cub in me."

"You think I don't know that?" he snarls. Before I know it he's in my face, teeth white and snapping close. "You think I don't live with the guilt of that every day? It's killing me, Denali." His hands grip my arms, shaking me. "But I can live with it. What I can't live with is knowing my lion hurt you." His grip loosens. "What if he hurts Nolan? I need to separate myself from you two, as much as it kills me."

"You wouldn't do that." My throbbing face and arms bely my conviction.

"*I just did.*"

"You didn't mean to—you were in a flashback."

"I know. But I'm always in flashbacks. I don't know what I'm capable of. I walked into that lab a man and a shifter. I became... something else. They made me something else."

"You can get help," I say shakily. "You can try—"

"I *am* trying, goddammit. This," he indicates the spoiled bed, "was me trying. It's not going to work."

I swallow back the grief rising. Pressure builds behind my face, burns my eyes. Is he really walking out on us? "What do I tell Nolan, when he wakes up and you're not here?" If my voice sounds wobbly, it's for Nolan, not me.

"I don't know." Nash bows his head. He doesn't turn around. "Tell him... his father is dead."

Nausea rocks through me, thick and heavy.

"Then go." Pain makes my voice harsh. "Leave us. It's not like we weren't fine before. You're the one who chose to show up. I knew I shouldn't have let you in."

Nash shakes his head. "You're right. You shouldn't have." He turns and walks out.

My bludgeoned heart falls to the floor where he stood a moment before.

## 12

# Nash

*Cold light. Grey light. I lie on the floor. My body tingles with agony. The last time they took me out of here, I lost consciousness after the first pain test. I don't know how long they worked me over, but I did nothing to resist. They threw me back in here and I haven't moved, not even when they shoved food inside. That could've been a day, or a week ago. The food smells wrong, as if it's started to turn.*

*Denali is gone. I couldn't protect her. As far as I'm concerned, I deserve to rot.*

*The door opens and the air wafts over me, heavy with the scent of antiseptic cleansers.*

*"This is your prize, your King of the Beasts? He does not look long for the world." A voice with a thick accent, a scent of a wolf I don't recognize.*

"The experiments have taken their toll." This voice I know. Smyth. The doctor in charge of the program. "But he still is a strong specimen. Former special ops. His lion emerged when he engaged in human battle. He was separated, pinned down, and his lion took over. Took twenty bullets. Slew every one of the enemy. A natural born killer."

"But now," the accented voice tinges with disdain. "He is quite pathetic."

"He formed an attachment with one of the breeders. A lioness. We think he mate marked her."

"Really? Where is she?"

"She escaped, sir. Some laziness with the guards. They had her uncuffed and she killed one, maimed the other. We tried to track her, but she's highly intelligent, and very determined. Took to the sewers—the trail disappeared."

"I wonder... if you found her, and returned her to him, would he revive?" The door closes, the voices muffled.

*No.*

I roll, stifling a groan, and drag myself to the food tray. I dip my fingers in the slop and eat. The gruel is tasteless, the meat almost spoiled, but I force it down. By the time I'm done, my body is on fire. The food does its work—giving my system what it needs to regenerate. I'll heal and co-operate and pretend I'm fine. If they ask me about the mate mark, I'll say it was an act of violence. That it meant nothing. I'll lie and do whatever ever they want me to do. Submit. Obey. Even if it drives my lion mad.

I have to live... if not for my sake, then for Denali's.

∽

Denali

. . .

THREE DAYS LIVING LIKE A ZOMBIE. I don't even know how I go through the motions with my clients, with Nolan. I broke down crying when Nolan asked where Nash had gone. My little boy wrapped his arms around my neck and squeezed, doing his best to offer me comfort.

"Don't cry, momma. He'll be back."

I shook my head. "No. He won't, Nolan. I'm sorry, baby, but he's not well enough to be with us. His lion is sick."

With the perceptiveness of a child, he corrected me. "No, momma. His lion is only sick when he's away from us."

I'd cried even harder then but threw myself into the shower to get it together.

Now, the two of us are hanging out in the backyard. He's playing with a dump truck. I'm staring at the same stain on the patio. I force myself to get up and turn on the hose to water the trees.

Fates, this pain in my chest. This heaviness.

I wish Nash had never come. I wish he hadn't made me fall in love again. To start to believe I could have that perfect life I dreamed of.

I understand he isn't well. I know he's afraid he might hurt me the way his father attacked his mom. But even so, I will never, ever forgive him for inserting himself into my life and then walking away.

∽

*AGENT DUNE*

NASH LEFT the cottage up in Temecula, but some gut instinct has Charlie still watching it. There's a child there, and he looks like Nash. Charlie can't find much on the mother, Denali, except that she disappeared from New Orleans four years ago and then resurfaced with the child, Nolan, only recently in California.

Charlie hides his car a mile away and hikes up around the hillside toward the back of the cottage. From the distance, he can see the child playing in the fenced backyard. Denali's out with him, watering with a hose. An unmarked white van pulls up in front of the cottage. Something about it strikes him as odd.

Denali says something to the boy and goes inside. The boy's head jerks up and then he falls to the ground, limp as a rag doll. A man vaults over the fence and drops right in front of him. He picks the boy up and tosses him over the fence, where another man catches him and runs to the van. The entire operation takes all of thirty seconds.

Charlie sprints down the hillside, his instinct to protect the innocent stronger than the need to gather intel, but it's too late. Both men are in the van and it's driving off.

He falls to his belly on the ground and yanks out his camera, snapping pictures of the van and the license plate as it peels around the corner and disappears.

Fuck.

His vehicle is way too far away to give chase. He turns and slips back up the hill.

In his career as a special ops agent he's seen and heard many terrible things. He's killed for his country. Committed and covered up crimes for his country. But nothing's made him as sick as hearing Denali's anguished screams echo up the mountainside when she realizes her son is missing.

∽

NASH

"ALPHA? ALPHA?"

"Not your alpha," I mumble, groping for my glass. My fingers hit a bottle and I lift that instead, gulping down the cool fire like it's water.

"Jay-sus," Declan breathes. He, Laurie and Parker lean over me. "Ya smell like a turpentine factory. What is that shite?"

I blink, pushing up from the bar to look groggily around the empty upper room at The Pit. I must've driven straight here after Denali kicked me out. I drank all night and most of the morning to forget. Even now my lion is charged up, burning the alcohol out of my system, demanding I go back and claim what's rightfully mine.

Except I don't deserve Denali. I don't deserve a family, much less a mate.

"Steady," Laurie murmurs, slipping behind me.

"'S good. I'm fine."

"Your eyes are red. Like, glowing. I've never seen this before."

"Lion," I rasp through cracked lips. "Wants out."

"Get him some water. And steak. Raw," Parker orders and turns back to me. "Fuck, Nash. What'd you do? Where's Denali?"

"Left her. Can't be with her. Can't be her mate."

"What about Nolan?"

I shake my head. "I'm too fucked up to raise a kid."

"You don't know that's true," Parker contradicts softly. He leans on the bar next to me. "So you're just going to stay away?"

I shrug. My lion won't let me. He'll fight to go back and drive me mad. I should chain myself up now.

"Should've stayed in the cell," I shiver, suddenly chilled. "Should've left me there to rot."

"Hang on, boss," Parker murmurs. "We'll figure a way out of this." He goes behind the bar and hands me a two-liter bottle of water. I drink the whole thing, but when Declan and Laurie return and set a plate of steaks near me, I shake my head.

"You gotta stay strong. At least long enough for us to figure out what to do when your lion takes over."

"Call Sam. His mate will know what to do." She worked at Data-X, she can cook up something deadly. Barring that, Sam can rig explosives and blow me to bits.

"All right. We'll make a plan." Parker pushes the plate close, and the smell of meat convinces me faster than anyone could. By the time I demolish the plate, I feel a little better. Maybe I can get Layne to dose me with something to make me forget. A few wolf packs use vampires to wipe the minds of anyone who threatens the pack. Supposedly it doesn't work on shifters, but maybe it'll be enough to forget how close I came to paradise.

Just the thought has me reaching for the bottle again.

*Denali.* A cracking sound and I open my hand to let the broken glass fall. Absently I pick a few shards out of my palm before my skin heals over them.

Parker takes a deep breath. "Boss—"

My phone rings and he falls silent as I reach for it. I stare at the name on the screen. I shouldn't answer. Leaving her gutted me. Talking to her now will ensure I never breathe again.

Except I'm so humbled she's even willing to dial my

number after what I did to her and Nolan, my thumb swipes across the screen.

"Nash?" The terror in Denali's voice jerks me to my feet.

"Denali."

Her sobs fill the line, breaking my heart.

"What—"

"They took him. Nolan. They came and took him."

Red fills my vision and I fight it. *Not now!*

"Who?" Parker and the rest huddle around me.

"Men in black. White van. I was in the back and didn't—" She's crying too hard to speak.

"Hang on, Denali, we're on our way," Parker says. His voice is muffled, as if coming to my ears through glass. My vision narrows, and I stay very still, trying to keep control.

"Give me the phone," Laurie says, and pries it from my nerveless fingers. "Denali? Can you hear me? Do you think you're safe there? Is there somewhere you can go?" His murmur follows me as I stride to the Camaro. Parker and Declan reach there before me. We're squealing away before the doors close, before I even have time to breathe.

"Who could've done this? Who do you think it is?" Parker asks.

"Call Sam." Declan's hands white knuckle the steering wheel. The Camaro accelerates into a turn. "He can find out."

"Denali's unhurt," Laurie says. "I have her meeting us." He leans forward to give directions to Declan.

"Don't worry, Nash," Parker says. "I'm calling back up."

I barely hear him over the roaring in my ears. Rage fills me like nothing I've felt before, lava driven through my veins with the force of a hurricane. A second later, Laurie presses my phone into my hand. "Alpha, they want to hear from you."

"Nash?" Sam's voice comes over the line. "I've got Layne here, and Jackson and Kylie. What's going on? Is it Denali?"

The lava turns to ice.

"My son," I growl. "They took my son!"

# 13

# N*ash*

"I just went in to snag my phone—it was ringing. They grabbed him while I was inside and by the time I got out it was too late." Other than a raspy voice and tear-swollen eyes, Denali appears calm and composed as she relates the story for the umpteenth time. We're huddled in one of Sam's safehouses. He and his mate Layne flew up as soon as they heard the news, and more of their pack and friends are on standby, waiting for orders. Parker and Declan keep checking their phones and leaving to make more calls.

"Any idea who these guys were?" Sam asks.

"I know who." My lion's been trying to tell me for days now. *That's* why the flashbacks intensified. "There was another with Smyth. A business partner with a Spanish accent." If I close my eyes I can hear the rich cultured tones rolling over me. I can see the polished black dress shoes and tip of the cane.

"Santiago," Sam says grimly. "We got everyone last time, except that son-of-a-bitch."

"Who's Santiago?" Denali asks.

"He was the money," Sam announces. "Smyth had the vision. Santiago bankrolled the project."

"We had the genes," I add. "A decorated soldier and a strong lioness." I rub my face and dare a glance at Denali. Right now, she's trying to stay strong.

"Santiago won't hurt him," Sam says. "He's obsessed with creating clean shifter lines. He thinks Nolan is the start of that."

"There's a bit 'o good news," Declan murmurs.

"We'll get him." Sam stands as voices come to the door. Layne enters first, a petite Asian woman with a faint smell of chemicals. She worked in a Data-X lab until Sam blew it up. A huge wolf is behind her. Jackson—a successful businessman with an info security company. I rise as Jackson approaches me. He's huge, and dominant, his wolf lighting his eyes. My lion is very aware of him and Layne—who's more dominant than she looks.

"Nash." Jackson shakes my hand. "I've heard a lot about you. My mate and I will put every resource we have at your disposal." He nods to Denali, including her.

"Thanks," I say.

I'm so fucking humbled. I've done nothing for any of these guys and yet they're all here to help me.

"Kylie is already searching the cyber underground for any sign of Santiago's men," Layne murmurs from the corner.

"We have a helicopter and private jet ready as soon as we have news."

"Thank you." Denali lets out a shaky breath. I nod, unable to speak. In the tight space, my animal isn't happy about so many alphas near my vulnerable mate.

Not that she's my mate anymore. I thoroughly fucked that up when I abandoned her and left our cub defenseless against the monster who stole him.

"I'm going to go help Kylie," Jackson says, and Layne follows him out of the room.

"These are your friends?" Denali asks in a whisper.

I shrug. "Friends of friends." I tighten my fists to keep from reaching for her. I need to touch her, but she shook off my touch when I first arrived. I don't want to push it.

The door opens again, and a woman slips in. Petite, blonde, human. A wolf enters with her, another giant, dominant male with tattoos on his hands and crawling up his neck. He hovers over the human female, who shares his scent. She also bears his mark.

"Denali?" The woman comes straight to my mate, kneels and takes my mate's hands. "I'm Amber." She looks up from her non-threatening position with eyes filled with compassion and some of the tension to leaks out of the room. "I'm here to help find Nolan."

My mate swallows. "How?"

Amber glances at the big wolf before answering. "I'm psychic. I... see things sometimes. Flashes of people's experiences."

"Amber has a gift," the big wolf says softly. His tattooed hand brushes her hair and Amber seems to draw strength from his touch.

The psychic draws in a breath. "Do you have anything of Nolan's here? A piece of clothing or something?"

"I do," Laurie says when no one speaks up. The skinny

shifter ambles forward, offering a little toy car. "The wheel fell off and he gave it to me to fix."

"He must like you," Denali whispers, tears gathering in her eyes. "It's his favorite." Her body shakes a little and I put my arm around her. She lets me this time. "All right." Amber takes the toy and cups it in her hand. "Can you tell me a little about Nolan?"

Denali's shaking intensifies. She's trying, and failing, to hold it together.

"We'll leave you two alone," Parker murmurs. He, Declan, and Laurie head for the door. I stand, not sure what to do. Amber immediately takes my place, leaning close to my mate and murmuring with her.

"Nash." The big wolf offers his hand to shake. "Just wanted to introduce myself. I'm Garrett, alpha of the Tucson pack. I've got the top guys in my pack here. As soon as we get intel, we're all ready to fly to find Santiago and fight."

I can barely nod with gratitude.

Garrett cracks his knuckles. "It's about time we went after Santiago. He had my sister kidnapped last year. Her mate is alpha in Mexico, where Santiago had his headquarters for many years. They haven't seen anything of him since he escaped when it all came out."

Sam slips in and glances at the two females. "Anything?"

"Not yet," Garrett says in a low voice. Just then Amber sucks in a breath, tilting back her head, eyes closed.

Sam holds out his phone recorder and catches Garrett's eye, waiting for the big wolf to nod before he kneels close to Amber and turns the recorder on.

"Lots of emotion in here," Amber mumbles. "Lots of people who care about Nolan. Eyes still closed, she holds out her hand and Denali takes it.

"I sense him. He's frightened, but safe. Men in black, with guns." A slight smile crosses her lips. "I think he's in cub form, so he can bite them if they get too close. I see cage bars—they're keeping him locked up. But he hasn't been hurt."

Denali goes limp like a puppet whose strings have been cut. Her head drops against her and Amber's hand. I move to squeeze Denali's shoulder, and she grabs my hand with her free one.

The contact with her runs through me like a jolt of electricity, energizing, harmonizing. My head clears, focus sharpens.

"They're speaking in Spanish. They're saying…" Amber falls silent and I fight the urge to demand she tell us what they said. I sure as hell hope she speaks Spanish. As the seconds tick by, her forehead creases. She twitches a little and whimpers. "No—" She ducks her head and raises her arms to protect herself. A few seconds pass.

"Amber?" Garrett rumbles. His own temples are wet with sweat.

The human blows out a breath and lets her arms down with a sigh. "They tranqued him. They're moving him somewhere. I heard one of the guards say Honduras." Amber sags. Garrett lifts her, and she curls up in his arms, pressing against his giant body.

"It's okay, baby," he murmurs. "You did good." He looks at Sam. "You got all that?"

"Yeah." Sam rises. "Jackson and Kylie are sweeping the darknet for anything they can find. I'll tell them."

"Thank you," I tell Amber and Garrett. The wolf nods and carries his half-conscious mate from the room.

"Oh my God." Denali lets out a breath. The tears she's

bravely kept at bay track down her cheeks. I wrap her in my arms.

Parker and Declan return, carrying bags of food. "Time to fuel up." They pass around packs of meat.

I accept my share, ripping open the package and taking a bite of raw steak.

"Garrett's gang went to four grocery stores and cleaned them out," Parker tells me. "Jackson is still working on getting coordinates with Kylie, but Amber's intel helped. The jet is almost ready. We'll head to Garrett's brother-in-law's place in Mexico, treat that as HQ."

I gulp down a mouthful of beef. "All right. After this we'll roll out."

"I'll spread the word."

"Parker." I catch his arm before he leaves. "Thanks." I turn to Declan and Laurie who are waiting by the door. "You too. I can't—" my throat closes. "I can't thank you enough."

"You got it," Declan says. "Alpha."

"Alpha," the other two echo, and for once, I let the title stand.

~

*Denali*

I CAN'T BREATHE. Can't think. The trip to Mexico City is a blur. We arrive past dark and drive a couple hours up to Garrett's sister's place.

Sedona, Garrett's youthful sister, greets us on the steps of the palatial hacienda and leads us to a suite of rooms. She's a wolf, like most of them, and her scent has a tinge of breastmilk to it. She has a nursing pup.

"Carlos is meeting with his pack. They all want to fight."

"My best fighters are on their way," Garrett tells her after a big hug. "Kylie's doing her best to find Santiago's trail in Honduras. Between her intel and Amber's visions, we should have a location soon."

Sedona shows us to our rooms. Amber and Garrett claim one immediately—the human looks dead on her feet. Laurie, Parker, and Declan have disappeared, and after kissing my forehead, Nash heads out, probably to talk to Jackson and Carlos.

"Is there anything I can bring you?" Sedona asks, and I realize she's talking to me. We're standing in a beautiful bedroom that I have no energy to appreciate. My ears are filled with cotton, my whole body numb.

"I'm fine. I should try to sleep. I couldn't on the plane."

She grimaces sympathetically, touches my shoulder and leaves me alone.

I lie down, but toss and turn, dropping off for a few minutes or so before rising. My lioness wants to prowl. I pad down the hallway, stopping by a half open door. A screen flickers on the far side of the room—footage of some sort. A cell. Whoever's watching fast forwards until a prisoner comes into view. I stifle a gasp. It's Nash—but not as I've ever seen him. He's barefooted, bare-chested in ragged fatigues. Body ravaged, emaciated. A shell of the soldier he once was and the fighter he is now. He looks half dead, but for those burning amber eyes.

Breathing hard, I push the door open.

"Denali?" Sam rises from where he was watching the screen. "I didn't know you were there."

"Is that—?"

"Footage from Data-X. I'm rewatching for clues." The young wolf looks exhausted. No—haunted. I try to remember what Nash told me, but all his friends are blending together. Was Sam a prisoner of Data-X, too?

"What did they do to him?"

Sam shrugs. "Testing. Torture." He absently rubs his arm, wincing as if in pain. "Smyth tried to push the limits of the shifters in his experiments."

"You were there, too," I guess. I know Sam's the connection with the Tucson pack. It fits.

His eyes are ancient in his youthful face. "Yeah."

We look at each other. There's nothing more to be said, because we both lived through it. So did Declan and Laurie and Parker. That's why they stick close to Nash. We've all been irreparably damaged by Data-X.

My glance flicks back to the image of Nash. I should've gone back for him. I'll never forgive myself. "I..." I clear my throat. "I didn't know it got that bad."

"He's tough. He survived."

"Not all of him." This is what he's been fighting. My vision blurs.

"You lose a part of yourself when you're tortured. When someone tries to reduce you to nothing." Sam turns off the screen, but it's too late. Nash's image is burned into my mind forever.

My chest heaves, my lungs like a bird fluttering, trying to take flight from a snare. Everything in me hurts so bad. Our cub missing. My mate damaged, possibly beyond repair.

"I didn't go back. I was pregnant and so scared. I had no one. It was all I could do to survive." Even as I repeat my excuses they fall flat, but Sam touches my arm.

"*No*. Going back would've been suicide. I waited and planned for years before I went back for my revenge and I had no one to lose. Not until I met Layne."

"You're the one who blew up the labs?"

He nods.

"With Nash?"

He hesitates. "I freed Nash. Then he helped me find Smyth."

He freed Nash. That's what I should've done. "How do I help him?"

"You don't do anything. Just be. Be who you are. Be his mate."

My hand goes to my shoulder, gripping the healed mark hidden under my shirt. "I don't know if I can."

"You can," Sam says. "I'm sure you can. If I can heal, so can he." Somehow, I believe him. He's young, but he just found his mate, Layne. "He's broken, Denali. His spirit is fractured, but he just needs his missing pieces. You know what they are?"

I nod. "His son, and his mate." *Nolan...and me.*

∼

AGENT DUNE

IT'S COMPLETELY FUCKING out of character for him to let anything get personal. Yes, the search for the secret of the labs was personal, but it was more of a gnawing curiosity. A need to understand his past.

It never detoured into caring about something. Desiring a certain outcome.

But somehow, somewhere, he aligned with these misfits. These people who have been experimented on and turned into wolves. Or were they werewolves to begin with and the government was studying them?

Either way, he picked sides. He chose them.

And they were missing one of their own. A small, defenseless child.

And he fucking stood there and watched it happen.

So yeah, it's now become his duty to get that boy back.

He calls Agent Gray. "What do you have for me?"

"You're applying a lot of pressure for someone who's asking a favor."

"A little boy got kidnapped." There. He went for honesty for a change. "I need to get him back."

He hears Gray draw in a breath. Agents don't know much about other agent's lives. That's on purpose. But he always suspected Gray had kids and that's why she didn't work in the field.

The clacking of her rapid fire key typing comes over the line. "I have a location on Santiago. It was redacted but I found a way in. He has a villa in Honduras, near La Ceiba. I'm sending the coordinates. He departed the U.S. for Honduras yesterday on a private jet, but there's no record of a boy. Of course, a kid would be easy to hide."

"Right. Thank you."

"You need help getting there?"

He smiled. "No. This is what I do best."

"That I know. Good luck, Dune."

In all the years she'd been his handler, she'd never wished him luck. "Thanks, Gray. I might need it."

"Dune?"

"Yeah?"

"Someone else has been trying to get into that information—searching for Santiago. An outsider—a hacker on the darknet."

A flush of knowing runs through him.

*The wolves.*

"Let them in."

She draws an audible breath. "Okay."

Damn. Either Agent Gray also knows their government is on the wrong side of this story, or she has way more trust in his decisions than he would've thought.

He ends the call and grabs his things. Time to head to Central America.

## 14

# N *ash*

I'm in a room full of wolves. Half are huge tattooed bikers, the other half brawny miners murmuring to each other in Spanish.

My motley pack is at my back.

"Kylie hacked the government files. We have the coordinates for Santiago's villa. Here." Jackson points to a satellite view map. "From what it looks like, a private compound near a landing strip outside La Ceiba."

"Nash," Jackson calls. "What do you think? You're lead on this." I know what the words cost him. His wolf is more dominant than any I've ever met. Almost too dominant to run a pack. Maybe that's why he focuses his energy into running a billion-dollar company.

I straighten as all eyes fall on me. My lion is calm. He's relishing the chance to spill enemy blood, but more than that, he wants to be in charge. It makes sense—I'm the one with a military background. I haven't used battle strategy in years, but it's all right here, easily accessible. "We attack in waves. The first line will take out as many guards as they can by stealth. When the alarm is sounded, we switch to a full-scale attack to breach the compound. The helicopters will provide cover."

Around me, wolves nod.

"Garrett, you'll lead the second wave. Sam, is there a way we can signal him to start the attack?"

"We can get intel," Sam says at the same time Laurie speaks up, "I'll do it."

"That'll work," I approve. "Carlos, your men know the jungle. I need a handpicked contingent for the first wave."

Carlos nods, yellow eyes gleaming. Of all the wolves here, he and his men most desire revenge. I have no doubt the Mexican alpha will be on the front lines.

"I'll be the first inside," I say. "I'll scent out Nolan if I can, but my priority is Santiago."

"You want him dead or alive?" one of Garrett's wolves asks.

"Muerto," a Mexican wolf mutters.

"We keep Santiago alive until my son is found. After that, I'm happy to turn him over to you and your men, Carlos." I smile enough to show my canines as approving mutters break out around me.

"Before we break into groups, let me say this." I wait until the room goes quiet. "I'm a soldier. I never asked to be alpha. I never thought I would lead." I glance at Jackson, who nods. He knows what it's like to be deadly and dominant.

"But there's only so much a man can take. I'm not a man. I'm a lion. A man-eater." I get a few startled looks at that admission. I sweep the room and Garrett returns my stare. I'm sure he exacted revenge on the men who kidnapped his sister. He knows the price of freedom, of keeping loved ones safe. "I've spent years suppressing that side of myself and let evil spread. But no longer.

"The evil has been rooted out, but there's one final stronghold. We've waited long enough." The shifters nod in unison as I declare, "It's time to go to war."

~

*Denali*

I STRIDE out to the Jeeps in front of the hacienda, past the waiting wolves. They're loading up, getting ready to head to the landing strip and fly out to Santiago's place. As soon as Nash sees me he heads my way.

I meet him boldly, squaring off with him. "Layne just told me the plan. I'm coming with you."

Instead of answering, Nash takes my hand and draws me aside. I wait until we're a ways away from the rest of the group to repeat myself. "I don't care what you think. I'm coming with you."

Nash nods. I'm not fooled. The minute he thinks my guard is down, he'll lock me in a dungeon to make sure I'm safe. I'm told the hacienda has one.

"Nash. I'm a lioness. I'm a fighter too. Besides, no one knows Nolan's scent like I do." I want to curl into a ball and weep at the thought of my little boy in the hands of these madmen. "He's my son."

"He's mine too. My priority is to keep you safe."

I don't spit his last words back. This is a new Nash. He's

changed. Whatever his issues with stepping into his rightful role, he seems to be over them.

"I'll be smart. I can hang back until it's time to find Nolan."

"All right."

My breath leaves in a rush. "So I can come?"

"Denali, if there's something you really want, I don't think I could ever deny you."

I sag, and he's there for me, holding me. I didn't let him touch me earlier. I couldn't take it. This man broke my heart into a million pieces. But as much as I want to be angry, I need him so much right now. And he's being everything I need him to be.

"I tried so hard to keep him safe," I choke out. "I hid as long as I could."

"Shhh, baby. It's not your fault," he says in a way that tells me he thinks it was his.

"It's not yours, either."

"My lion was trying to warn me. That's what all my flashbacks were. I should've been there. I should've kept you safe."

I can't speak, so I hug him.

His lips find my ear. "Baby, if you give me another chance, I swear, I'll never walk away again." He steps back and holds my shoulders. *"Ever."*

Tears swim in my eyes. Will I take him back?

It would be impossible not to. If Nolan and I are the missing part of him, he's the missing part of me.

I nod, and he thumbs away the tears tracking down my cheeks. "Yes, you'll take me back?"

My head wobbles on my neck, but I manage to nod.

Nash holds my face and leans his forehead against mine. "Thank fuck," he breathes. His jaw sets when he pulls away.

"I will get our son back," he swears with the timbre of an oath.

"I know you will," I whisper. I believe Nash would move mountains to make it happen. He'll get our Nolan back.

He has to.

∼

*NASH*

As soon as the helicopter lands, I'm on the ground. Another day, another jungle. Memories of my soldier days rise and flash through my mind. But no flashbacks. For the first time in decades, my mind is clear.

My lion is quiet, biding his time. He knows I'll let him out soon. He was born for this. Not a monster. A warrior, born for battle. Born to protect my own. An alpha.

We assemble about a mile out from the target. Everyone's quiet, readying for battle. Denali stands nearby, staring into the underbrush. She's so beautiful, her face composed. She wears dark, loose fitting clothes. As soon as we get close, she'll let loose her lioness. Despite everything, I'm looking forward to seeing her animal again.

Jackson walks by and I lean close to him. "I have a favor to ask." I jerk my chin toward Denali. "Watch her?"

"Every step of the way." He grips my shoulder briefly. Shifters touch more than humans do, but I've heard Jackson is a notorious loner. He found Sam after Sam escaped from Data-X as a teenager. Jackson took him in and Sam was the only one close to him until Kylie.

"Ready, Alpha?" Parker and Declan appear at my side. They're about to strip down and take wolf form. They insisted on fighting, and I didn't try to talk them out of it but ordered them to come in with Garrett. I sense they want to stay close to me.

I grip their shoulders. "You have Nolan's scent. I need you to be on the lookout for him."

"Aye, boss."

"Thank you."

Above our heads, an huge owl swoops onto a branch and settles. My radio crackles.

"I've got eyes on the compound," Sam says. "Layne is staking out now."

"Got it." I signal everyone. "We're moving out."

～

*Nash*

Santiago's mansion is a quiet, sprawling shadow, lying between the jungle and the sea. We approach from the jungle side and wait for our moment in the darkness along the high wall.

"No moon tonight," Carlos murmurs. "And the wind's blowing off the sea. Any guards who are also shifters won't scent us coming." Above our heads, the leaves stir restlessly in the wind. "We better move soon."

"On my signal." I step forward. I call my lion and let my hands turn to paws. Carefully, I climb the compound wall. Manicured lawns stretch before me. From Laurie and Layne's scouting, I know there are gun-wielding guards at every possible exit or defensible spot of the compound, including a few pacing the perimeter.

The great white owl dives on silent wings above my head

and I give the signal before leaping onto the lawn. The wolves follow, breaching the walls easily enough. There are a few startled cries along the forest line as the wolves leap from the shadows and take out the first line of guards. Black clad bodies hit the ground simultaneously.

We now have a matter of minutes to infiltrate the mansion. But first we have to cross the lawn without getting caught.

Gun balanced on my shoulder, I creep forward with the line of advancing wolves.

∼

*Denali*

"They're in," Sam reports.

"Roger," Garrett replies via walkie talkie, rising along with his wolves. "We're ready."

"Roger, wait for my signal."

For a few tense moments, we wait in silence, the wolves giant statues, shirtless in readiness to shift. A breeze rustles through the trees and the shifting shadows play over the tattooed muscles.

A shout, and gunfire clatters in the distance.

The walkie talkie crackles. "Cover blown. Go, go, go!"

I surge to my feet, letting the lioness take my skin. I claw up the wall and hit the lawn at a dead run. Ahead of me, wolves race, noses pointed toward the hacienda, tails streaming. A flash of white from the left. I duck my head until I realize it's Laurie, his large feathered form swooping in. Sparks flash as he draws gun fire. A yelp ahead of me, and a wolf goes down. The rest run faster, reaching the low wall of the mansion and leaping over it. More gunfire blasts but it's too late. Garrett's pack is among the guards, a swarm of deadly shadows.

More gunmen rise up on a parapet, hoisting weapons, but wolves appear behind them before they can fire.

A giant wolf, almost big as a lion, slams into them, casually knocking them to the waiting wolves below. I recognize him as Tank, second in Garrett's pack, and dominant enough to lead a pack himself, if he wanted.

Hugging the wall, I duck into an alcove and wait for the wolves to make short work of the enemy.

I need to focus on finding Nolan.

I shift back to human form. Beside me, Jackson does the same. From the way he's dogging my steps, I know Nash put him on me. My own personal guard wolf.

"Intel says there's a west wing of the house with extra security. If I had to guess, I'd say that's where he is."

I nod.

More gunfire and a howl goes up. A second later I duck my head at an explosion. Bits of debris rain against the wall.

"I thought we said no explosives until we find Nolan!" I cry. "Who brought the grenades?"

Jackson shakes his head.

"Incoming!" someone cries, and the building shakes with another blast. "That's right! Fuck you, muthafuckas," a young woman's voice blasts out on a loudspeaker.

Jackson makes strangled noise. "Kylie." His face is stricken.

It takes me a second to remember that's the name of his mate. "What? She's here?"

"She can't be," he chokes out. He rises, staring through the smoke and ash.

"Go," I told him. "Find her. I'll be fine."

Another explosion and Kylie whoops in victory along with Garrett's wolves. He dashes out and disappears.

"Fuck this," I mutter, and shift back into the lioness. The battle has moved—the explosions growing more distant. Tail weaving, I pad forward, nose to the ground, trying to pick up my son's scent.

The walls shake as I prowl down a marbled hall, stopping only when men shout and booted feet slam through rooms nearby. The rat-tat-tat of machine gunfire is constant. Passing through one room filled with dead gunmen, I find a set of bloody paw prints and follow them toward the scent of acrid gunpowder, and the smell of the sea.

As I near the back of the mansion, the boom of big guns grows louder. I run faster, slinking along the wall below the level of smoke. I skid into a hall, and jerk as someone opens fire on me. My paws slip on the polished stone. I retreat just in time to avoid the bullet spray. Marble shards bite through my fur and I howl in pain. Something lands by me and explodes. I roar at the flash of pain in my eyes. Blinded, I scramble backwards and hit the wall. Shit. If the gunman follows, he'll pin me down, no problem.

Through streaming eyes, I see him stalk forward through the smoke. I roll as the gun blasts and hits a heavy piece of furniture. Gunfire follows me, tearing through wood, sending splinters into my body.

A flash of black and orange, and a cat scream, and the gun goes abruptly silent. I hear a growl, and a shadow whirls on me. The smoke clears, and I realize a tiger just saved me. Layne. She swishes her tail and turns on her prey.

Finding my feet, I lope away.

Nolan. I have to find Nolan. I search but can't catch his scent among the smells of battle.

Then my lioness catches it. Subtle, snaking through the halls. It's everywhere, but stronger the closer to the sea I get.

Not Nolan's scent. Santiago's.

I lope forward, fur prickling as I hear the chop, chop, chop of a helicopter's blades.

A sound rips through the mansion, and I break into a run, racing toward the lion's roar.

I burst onto a giant balcony, surrounded by lush jungle, overlooking a turquoise sea. Paradise.

A helicopter hovers on the edge of the stone parapet. A black flock of gunmen surround a figure climbing in. Santiago.

Guns blast from the roof, pinging the helicopter. A few gunman fall but Santiago has already stepped into the helicopter even as it lifts off. He's getting away.

With all the strength in my body, I rush over the balcony and leap off the edge.

∽

*Nash*

"Hold fire," I cry as the lioness darts from cover. Whirling, I rip the gun from the wolf's shoulder. "You might hit Denali!"

The air shudders under the helicopter's blades, carrying the sound of the lioness' outraged screams. A second later, two bodies fall from the helicopter to the balcony below.

"Who else is on that copter?" I demand.

"Three men. I don't see any kids," the wolf beside me with a pair of binoculars reports.

"Then shoot it down." I shove the gun back at the wolf

and leap from the roof on to the flagstones below. As soon as I land I race to my mate. Santiago sprawls nearby, blood leaking from a cut on his head. I ignore him.

"Denali?"

The lioness lies on her side. She's magnificent, golden from head to paw. As I approach breath ripples through her body and she raises her head.

"Denali." I fall to my knees, unable to stop my hands running down her beautiful flank, checking for wounds.

A warning rumbles in her throat, her eyes widening at something behind me.

I throw myself over her body just before the drumbeat of gunfire. Bullets punch my Kevlar, driving me forward. A few bite into my legs and arms. Denali's body jerks as her legs are hit.

With a roar I turn, pulling power through my body. All day I could feel it gathering in me—a new dimension of strength. My pack. I called on the alpha ability now, and power rushes through me, filling me with heat. The stinging cuts on my body heal in the two strides it takes to reach Santiago. I kick the gun from his hands.

Santiago whimpers as I crouch by his broken body.

"My son," I growl. "Where is my son?"

"He's not yours," Santiago pants.

Denali snarls.

"Tell that to his mother." I nod to the angry lioness.

"She was just a breeder. The right combination of genes. That boy wouldn't exist if it weren't for me," the deranged old shifter cries.

After a few attempts, Denali surges to her feet and limps to my side. I bite back my warning for her to be careful. Blood streams from the wounds in her side but her eyes are bright. No vitals were hit.

"Do you remember her? Lioness. One word and she'll bleed you. And she won't rush it. She'll make it slow. Tell us where our son is." I drag him to the edge of the balcony and throw his torso over the edge.

Santiago yelps as his weight nearly tips and sends him to his death. At the last moment, I catch the back of his shirt to hold him balanced. "Tell us."

"He's here."

"Where?" I demand.

"Western wing," Santiago pants.

"All right." I yank him back from the edge and let his body drop to the marble floor. "Denali, let's go."

Santiago attempts to stand, but wobbles and falls.

"No, don't go anywhere, old man. Some of your old friends are dying to see you," I tell him. A growl sounds behind me. Carlos and his wolves slink at the mouth of the balcony, waiting for us lions to abandon our prey.

Santiago's skin goes ashen.

"If I were you, I'd try to run." I nod to the edge of the wall. It'll be a mercy if the drop kills him. I turn and hurry after my mate, following the trail of blood.

"Denali, wait!"

By the time I catch up, she's dragging herself forward, inch by painful inch.

"You're hurt. You need to get back."

She staggers, her head weaving back and forth.

I kneel and put my hand on her shoulder. "Shift," I order. The lioness disappears in a rush. A bullet clinks to the floor, Denali's body shudders a little with the transformation, but her wounds look better. I enforced the command with alpha power—something I've never used before. Didn't even know I had. I strip off my shirt and cover her.

"I'm fine." She winces as I help her sit up.

"No, you're not."

"Found them," a young woman's voice rings out. A black drone appears, hovering in the air. "Here they are!"

"Nash—Denali—thank fates." Jackson rushes in. "Did you find him?"

"Santiago," I confirm. "Carlos has him." Or what's left of him.

"I have a reading on a highly alarmed room, on the second story in the west wing of the house," the drone chirps. "I think it might be Nolan."

Denali grips my hand.

"I'll get him," I say. "First let's get you to the helicopter."

"Not leaving Nolan," she grits.

"Please, baby. I can focus better on getting Nolan if I know you're safe. *Please.*"

"I've got her," Jackson says. "You go with Kylie."

"Kylie?"

"Right here." The drone zooms closer. There's a tiny screen and a smiling woman waves at me. "You didn't think I'd miss out on the action, did you?"

Jackson mutters something about punishment as he crouches to let Denali throw her arm over his shoulders.

She gasps as he lifts her.

I hesitate.

"Nash, go," Denali urges.

I jog behind the drone. Kylie navigates deftly through the halls.

"There might be guards," she says. "Give me a moment."

I pause as she flies forward, then calls, cheerfully. "All clear."

We turn into a hall.

"Last door on the right, I believe," Kylie remarks. "This

mansion is pretty nice. For a psychopathic bad guy, Santiago had good taste. Nash—wait!"

I halt in my tracks. A little light beams from the drone, illuminating little red lines crisscrossed in front of the door.

"Lasers," Kylie says. "Apparently Santiago didn't trust his own guards to watch your son. Can you get through?"

I nod and back up. Drawing on the lion's strength, I take a running leap and sail over the laser grid.

Normally I'd shift, but I don't want to break down the door if I don't have to. No need to scare my son.

My hand closes on the doorknob. It turns easily.

"Excellent," Kylie breathes. "I'll tell Sam to have the helicopter on standby."

After a moment my eyes adjust to the dim interior, I step inside. The room is large and surprisingly beautiful, a child's space filled with toys. A nursery for a beloved son.

Carlos told us Santiago was never able to have children. Maybe if he had, he would never have embarked on his quest to create a master race.

At the end of the room, there's a bed. As I approach, the blankets stir, and Nolan sits up, face sleepy.

"Nash?" he rubs his eyes. "You came for me."

"Yes," I go to my knees, and open my arms as he pushes off the bed and rushes to me. "Son."

*≈*

*Denali*

THE THROBBING in my side nearly blinds me.

"Get her out of here," Jackson calls.

"Wait!" I cry. "Please. Not without—"

"It's okay," Sam assures me. "Our position's secure. We've got time."

I gnaw my lip. What if there was another pocket of guards? What if Santiago did something with Nolan and he's locked up—or not here?

"Trust him, Denali."

A figure parts the mist of the predawn gloom. My lioness knows before I surge up from the seat.

Nash carries Nolan across the lawn. My boy's arms around my mate's strong neck, little face turned up to tell him something. Nash answers and both look over at me. I catch my breath.

"Momma," Nolan cries as soon as he sees me. I'm crying, arms reaching for him. Nash closes the distance and hands him to me.

"He's fine," Nash reassures as I bury my face in Nolan's hair, breathing in his scent. I check my boy over as Nash straps us both in carefully.

"Mom, why are you crying? I'm okay. Nash came for me."

"I know, baby."

"Ready?" Sam calls from the pilot seat.

"All set," Nash tells him. "Ready for takeoff. Take my family home."

∼

*Agent Dune*

Charlie lowers the scope of the sniper rifle and rolls to stand up. A crack of a twig has him snapping the gun back to his shoulder, whirling and aiming to shoot. Just as quickly, he lowers the muzzle.

It's a wolf. One of them.

A shudder of recognition runs through him, just as it did when he watched the group of humans shift and change. Not all of them are wolves. Nash is a lion and so is his girlfriend. He saw a tiger and an owl, too.

The wolf lifts its upper lip in a growl, showing its teeth.

Knowing there's a human behind the fangs, Charlie drops the gun and lifts his hands. "Easy. I just came to make sure you got the boy back. I'm not part of this operation."

The wolf advances, still growling.

A week ago, he might have shot the wolf first and asked questions later, but not now. Not after what he just saw. After what he felt.

Watching the men change into animal form did something strange to his body. His cells heated and rearranged, like they knew the pattern. Like they wanted him to change, too.

"I'm not with Santiago. I gave you guys the coordinates to find this place."

The wolf launches itself at him.

He throws up his forearm to block the bite, but it never comes. The wolf knocks him to his back and stands on him but doesn't go for his throat.

In a flash, the wolf transforms into an angry man.

Charlie's nose smashes under a brutal punch from Jared Johnson, the fighter he picked up in Tucson.

"What do you know about the boy?" Jared demands.

Charlie uses his legs to throw Jared off him and springs to his feet, hands up at the ready. He has another gun at his hip, but he doesn't go for it. Jared isn't trying to kill him.

"I saw them take the boy." The two circle each other. Jared's fists are up like a boxer's. "I was too far away to stop it, but I felt obligated to follow up. Make sure you got him back."

Jared lunges in for a punch, but Charlie dodges it and slips back without retaliation. It might be the first time he's fought a naked man.

"You work for the government," Jared accuses.

"I'm not on the job."

"Why are you here?"

"I just told you."

Jared drops his fists as abruptly as he first attacked. "Bullshit." He lifts his chin. There's a challenge there that sends the prickles of ice up and down Charlie's spine. *"Shift."*

Charlie doesn't understand the command, but his body heats again, the queer sensation of cells moving and rearranging happening again.

*"Shift, asshole."* Jared's voice carries more power than it should.

It seems to echo in Charlie's ears, go through his torso. A twisting, wrenching, shattering sensation tears his body apart. His clothing grows too small and rips on his body, and then he's closer to the ground, staring down at a pair of giant, white paws. The pain in his broken nose disappears.

What... the *fuck*?

But even as his mind reels, some small inner voice whispers *I knew it.*

He lifts his head and stares up at the human.

There's a triumphant gleam in Jared's eye. He crosses his arms over his chest. "Is this what you really wanted to know? Hmm, Agent Dune?"

Of course, Charlie can't speak to answer. All he can do is growl.

"Shift back," he commands again.

Just as inescapably, his body transforms again. Charlie's

on his ass on the ground, his torn clothing twisted around his limbs.

"Stay off our trail. You want answers, come and ask me directly. You know where I live." And with that, Jared blurs and drops to all fours, loping off into the jungle on giant wolf paws.

Charlie lifts his hands and examines them. No trace of paws remains. "Well," he mutters aloud. "That was fucking weird."

An uncharacteristic smile creeps across his face and something, some animal part of him, celebrates.

A werewolf.

"No shit." He chuckles as he packs up his gun.

# 15

# N*ash*

"It's not like I was actually there," Kylie's voice crackles on the microphone. We're back at the hacienda and the place buzzes with excitement, even though plenty of wolves are getting treated for wounds. Denali and Nolan are safe in their suite—I left them to do the rounds and debrief with the alphas before bed.

"I wouldn't put myself at risk," Kylie continues. Sam has her on screen on his laptop, Jackson is bent over him, frowning at his mate. Kylie doesn't seem too concerned, examining her nails which are all lengthened to claws. "I couldn't just sit back and let you rush into danger without me there."

"Nearly gave me a heart attack when I heard your voice," Jackson growls and waves a hand around the room at

Garrett and his pack. "Do you see their mates rushing into battle?'

"Amber is human," Kylie points out. "And, knowing Tank, he chained his mate up so she wouldn't follow him."

"Tied her to the bed," Tank confirms, without looking up from the weapon he's cleaning.

"Nash." Sedona stands in the door, signaling me. A fat, beautiful baby sits on her hip, chattering away in baby language. I nod to both Garrett and Jackson and follow her out.

"Laurie, Declan, and Parker are asking about you, but I thought you'd want to see them."

"Thanks. How's Carlos and your pack?"

"Six wolves sustained bad wounds, but Carlos and most of them are fine." She suppresses a smile. "They've already started celebrating. I'm sure you'll hear them setting off fireworks later. The fiesta will probably last a week." She stops at a door and lowers her voice. "Layne and I checked them over and got their wounds cleaned up. Parker and Declan weren't shot, but Layne and Laurie found them passed out on the ground. Pulled them out of the action and got them back here."

"That was me," I say. "I got wounded defending Denali and called on the pack bonds to heal me up fast."

"I thought so," she nods. "Well, they're fine. Just a bit weak. We told them to rest, but they wanted to see you—"

"Of course."

She steps aside. I pause with my hand on the doorknob. "Sedona? Thank you."

I wait until she smiles and pads away before opening the door to a dimly lit room. Sedona's smart, hosting the wounded well away from the healthy members of a pack. It's not the nature of predators to show compassion to the weak. Sometimes blood just makes shifters think of meat.

Inside, Laurie sits with his arm bandaged. He's the only one sitting up. Parker and Declan lay on their beds, looking pale. They bore the brunt when I pulled power from the pack.

The three of them straighten as I enter.

"Don't get up," I order and they all relax. I grin to myself at the sight of them actually following my commands. Guess I really have taken on the mantle of Alpha now.

"How's Nolan?" Laurie asks.

"Safe," I confirm. "Healthy. Probably a bit shaken but he'll be fine. Denali's getting him to bed." My son couldn't stop talking about the helicopter ride. Apparently, Sam promised him flying lessons. Denali was not pleased.

"And Santiago?"

"Gone. Denali and I turned him over to Carlos."

My pack nods their approval. They know Carlos' pack had the biggest score to settle with the evil wolf.

"So what now?" Parker asks just as Laurie blurts, "Are you our alpha?"

"I've always been an alpha," I say. "I just didn't know it. I'd be honored to be yours."

"Alpha," Laurie and Declan mutter. Parker angles his head, showing his throat with a grin.

"I know I pulled some power from you during the fight." I squeeze Declan and Parker's shoulders and they relax even further. "You good?"

"All good, boss," Parker confirms.

Declan puts his hand over mine for a second, smiling weakly.

I tighten my grip, letting my strength flow into them. By

the time I take my hand away, their cheeks are flushed, and their eyes are brighter.

Parker struggles to sit up.

"Oh no you don't." Layne hustles into the room, pushing him back down. "You need to rest. I'll dose you with a sedative."

"Sleep," I order, and Parker and Declan's eyes close. Laurie's head droops and Layne helps him back onto the pillow.

"I'll stay with them," she whispers.

"Thank you," I tell her and slip out.

Whoops and shouts dog my steps as I head through the hacienda. The courtyard is full of shifters and the smell of meat. A Mexican wolf staggers past, grinning broadly and drinking something alcoholic straight from a dark jug.

"Amigo!" He toasts me, angling his head slightly in respect to my lion's dominance. I smile and wave off his offer to drink. I'm wide awake and pumped on adrenaline, but there's only one place I want to be.

I head toward the quieter part of the hacienda, hastening my steps until I come to the suite of rooms marked with familiar cinnamon scent. Denali and Nolan are inside. My family. I hesitate only a moment before I open the door.

The three rooms—two bedrooms adjacent to one sitting room—are dark. Denali sits on the bed in the smaller room, watching Nolan sleep. I lean against the doorframe and watch them both. My mate and son. My family.

Denali stands up and walks toward me. Even in the dark, I see her eyes glittering grey-blue. Her lioness is showing.

Hips swaying, she peels her t-shirt off over her head.

My cock punches out against my jeans. I force myself to

keep my arms at my sides, though. Denali's making the move. I'm going to let her.

"Have I told you how much it turns me on to see you fight?" She slides her hands up under my shirt, then digs her nails into my chest.

A snarly-purr issues from my throat. "I might have noticed last time." My voice is impossibly deep. I pull off my shirt to give her full access to my chest. She scrapes her nails over my nipples, clawing lightly down my hard abdomen.

She pushes me backward, out of Nolan's doorway and shuts the door behind us. One hand on my chest, one hand unfastening my jeans, she propels me into the other bedroom. "Mm hmm. I'm going to need some of this big lion cock tonight."

Lord help me. How could I ever have walked out on this spectacular female? I can't even contemplate what I would've given up.

The backs of my knees hit the bed and I sit down. Denali has my zipper down. She drops to her knees at my feet and frees my length.

It's all I can do not to bury my fist in her curls and fuck her lush mouth like a maniac. Instead, I squeeze my hands into fists at my sides, letting her drive.

And she definitely seems to have torture in mind, because she takes her time flicking her tongue around the head.

"Denali," I growl. "You're playing with fire."

She releases the head of my cock with a pop of her lips and smiles. "Oh yeah?" She bites my inner thigh. "How is that?"

"If you're not going to take my cock deep into that pouty mouth of yours, I'm gonna pin you to the floor and pound between your legs until you beg for mercy."

She kisses up my inner thigh, then sucks my balls.

My knuckles crack under the pressure of my clenched fists.

"You wanna show me who's boss?" she teases, turning her lips inside to shield her teeth as she pumps her mouth over just the tip.

I growl. "You have five seconds. Five... four..."

Her beautiful eyes widen and her gaze locks with mine, but she doesn't take me deep, keeps on teasing.

"Three-two-one," I rush and pick her up by her upper arms. I toss her onto the bed on her back and yank down her bra cups. I go to town on her right breast, sucking the nipple while I squeeze and knead the other breast roughly. She tears at my hair, claws my arms, her pelvis bucking up for friction.

I slide my hand down between her legs. "You showing me where you want my cock, baby? Or where you want my mouth?"

She arches up. "Your cock," she rasps.

"My cock? You sure?" I rub a knuckle against the seam of her jeans, working it against her clit. "I thought you wanted this slow." I graze her nipple with my teeth.

She rolls her head from side to side. "Not slow. No." She already sounds wanton and needy. I can't wait to make her scream.

"No?" I crawl lower and slowly peel her jeans off her legs.

She reaches her fingers into her panties, working them between her folds.

"Nuh uh." I grab her wrist and pin it beside her head. "That's my pussy. Only I get to touch tonight." With my free hand, I yank her panties off, tearing the fabric in my haste.

Denali moans and reaches with her legs to pull me in. I

chuckle because her legs are strong, and I can't hold down both her hips and her wrist. I roll her over and pin both wrists behind her back, then give a light slap to her ass. She moans again, and I want to slap it more, spank her harder, but I'm afraid of waking Nolan.

Instead, I pull her hips up until she rests on her knees and I taste her.

Fuck, yes.

That cinnamon mating scent of her lioness permeates the room, tingles on my tongue. I work my tongue between her lips, tracing along the inside, flicking against her clit. I make my tongue stiff and penetrate her.

She bucks and fights for control of her hands. "Nash... Nash."

"Not yet, baby. I'll fuck you when I'm good and ready. Right now, I need to taste your pussy."

"You *tasted* it," she moans. "Fuck me, already."

I slap her ass, then lick from clit to anus and back again. Her thighs tremble, breaths drag in and out with a shudder. I want to tease her all night, but I'm losing control, myself. The need to claim her is far too strong.

I shove my pants off. Denali waits in position, face pressed into the mattress, hands still held at her lower back. I have a condom in my wallet, but I don't go for it. Instead, I rub the head of my cock through her juices and say, "When you get this cock it's going to be bare-back, baby. Nothing between us. Because I missed you carrying my cub last time, and I'm dying to see what it looks like."

I wait, because I'm not really asshole enough to make that decision without her consent.

Denali rolls her head to the side to look back at me. "Y-you want more cubs?"

"Yeah. Do you?"

Denali rolls her face back to the mattress with a sob and I'm on top of her in a flash, both of us flattened against the mattress, my body blanketing hers.

"Baby. Talk to me. I'm sorry. What is it?"

She rolls under me and turns her wet face into my neck. "It's good," she chokes. "I'm happy." She sinks her teeth into my flesh, like she's marking me.

I jerk when her fangs punch through my skin, more out of surprise than pain. She laps the wound with her tongue as her hand slides between us and grips my cock. "Give me that lion cock," she purrs. "I'd have a million cubs with you."

Oh Christ. A lion's roar shakes the walls. I surge over her, plow in deep. She wraps her strong legs around my waist and pulls me in at the same time her arms twine around my neck and yank me down for a kiss.

I take her mouth with the same ferocity I claim her, lips bruising, tongue lashing between her lips. My hips thrust, sending me home, home, home with each spectacular stroke. I've never known bliss before this moment, and I'll never forget it—Denali, devouring me in equal measure, pledging her body and soul to me, to our family.

Happiness pours through my lion, who I embrace. We are one, working together to please our mate. No longer do I fear him or imagine he will hurt the people I love. It was only me hurting him that made me sick.

I ride Denali until we're both slick with sweat, gasping and panting. I never want to come, and yet I'll die if I don't. I can tell by Denali's keening cries, she's close, too. There's something more that's needed. Something I'm supposed to say.

"I'm yours, lioness. You marked me. I'll never leave your side again," I pledge.

She orgasms, nails digging into my back, pussy squeezing like a tight glove around my cock.

As soon as she starts, I go off, too. I slam in twice more before burying my cock deep inside her and releasing. I seem to come and come, as if my lion knows my intent was to breed her and he's released a lifetime of my essence to fill her.

Denali's still shaking beneath me and squeezing me, mouth closed on my shoulder again. I rock slowly in and out, caressing her battered channel with my manhood now.

"I haven't touched another since the day I met you." I want her to know. She's always been mine.

"Me neither," she whispers into my ear. "I've just been waiting for you all this time. I knew you'd come."

A shudder of rightness runs through me. I ease to my side and gather her against me, our bodies still connected. "I never should've held back. I just... didn't want to hurt you any more than I had."

"You never hurt me. All you did was protect and give. And look at the gift it became." She smiles in the direction of Nolan's room.

I stroke her curls back from her beautiful face. This time I kiss her softly. "All I did was rut and mark. You—" I stop because my eyes suddenly burn, and I have to blink. "You healed me."

Denali wraps herself around me, tightening her hold until our bodies become one living, moving thing. I breathe in our mingled scents. We're one now, an entity all on its own. There's an *us*. A *we*. After a lifetime of being alone, of pushing everyone away, I'm connected. To Denali. To Nolan. To my rag-tag motley pack of misfits. To their extended circle of friends who came through for me—no, for *us*—in our most dire hour of need.

It's unbelievable. And beautiful.

Living—my life—is a joy.

Thank fate. Thank God. Thank my lion. Thank Denali. Gratitude tumbles through me and out of me as I slip into my first peaceful night's sleep in ages. Maybe ever.

I am whole again.

# EPILOGUE

D*enali*

A BREEZE BLOWS through my kitchen, carrying the scent of wildflowers. They wave on the slope, thousands of them, multi-colored blooms that blossomed overnight, after the rains.

I stand barefoot at the counter, shifting my weight from side to side as I stir a batch of peanut butter cookies. The timer dings—the first batch is done. I set it out and give the dishcloth a little wave, sending the scent wafting out the screened door—a scent no man, or lion, can resist.

Sure enough, a few minutes later, two figures appear, striding back toward the house. Halfway down the slope, Nash stoops down and picks up our son. At four years old, Nolan's gotten big, but his dad has broad shoulders. Broad enough to bear my mark. Broad enough to bear our son... and soon, our daughter.

I smile wider as Nash pauses, bending carefully to pick a handful of wildflowers.

"These are your mother's favorite," he tells Nolan, handing them up for our boy to carry. I lean too close to the counter and Nadia kicks in protest.

I drop my hands to my rounded belly.

"Not long now," I whisper. Her father already calls her *princess*, just as he calls me his *queen*.

The pack calls Nolan *the little prince*, and they still call him *king of the beasts*—but only to tease him. He barely allows the pack calling him *Alpha*, though I think he likes it more than he lets on. But no, he insists he's just *Nash*. Or *Denali's mate*. Or, to Nolan, and soon Nadia, *daddy*.

He takes care of us all—his family and his pack.

We all continue to operate under the radar, just in case the government decides to come looking for any of us. But they've turned The Pit into something slightly more attractive—a biker bar style tavern called The Jungle—to serve as better cover for the fight club.

Nash fights, but only once a week. The rest of the time, he's handyman to me, the tavern, and now much of the neighborhood.

He's garnered fame as a fighter throughout all of North America and gets invited to all kinds of shifter games and events. Most of them he turns down. He won't leave me and Nolan again, not even for a night or two.

He and Nolan bump into the cottage, and Nolan presents me with the wildflowers. Nash sweeps around behind me and puts his hands on my belly, his lips on my neck. I lean back into him.

It's times like these I miss my family—my grandfather and aunt who raised me. I would've liked them to know how happy I am. How much of them I see in the way I parent.

The way I view life. But I can't dwell on my losses. Because my gains are too big.

I have Nash.

I have Nolan.

Soon, I'll have Nadia.

And together, we're our own pride.

No one will keep us down. Not ever again.

## RECIPE: EASIEST PEANUT BUTTER COOKIES EVER

*Renee's note: and they're gluten free!*

1 cup peanut butter
1 cup sugar
1 egg
1 tsp vanilla extract

Mix everything together. Roll dough into 1-inch balls and lay out on a cookie sheet. Flatten each ball with a fork in a crisscross pattern.

Bake for 10 mins at 325 degrees F and let completely cool before getting them off the pan. Eat or crumble on top of vanilla ice cream. :D

# AUTHOR'S NOTE

Lee here. I have to give a huge shout out to Renee, co-writer extraordinaire and awesome friend. This series wouldn't exist without her, not to mention this book. I pretty much handed over a bunch of scenes and an idea, and she did the rest. I read the results with tears in my eyes; she made the book what it was meant to be. She's magic.

I'm so incredibly grateful for this series. In each book I think we pushed the limits of our writing and storytelling abilities, while having more fun that should be legal. We have ideas for a lot more bad boy shifter books, so I hope you enjoy reading them half as much as we love writing them.

I want to dedicate this book to our kids, who make life amazing fun, challenging, and so much richer.

Thanks to the Bad Alpha Dad (BAD) authors, especially Gwen Knight, for inviting us to the group and for making Nash's original cover. Aubrey Cara, Alexis Alvarez, and Miranda for beta and editing services. Melissa for helping with my newsletter and Nanette helping with ARCs and the

Goddess Group. Our hubbies for helping with the kids while we write!

And huge thanks to Renee Rose for being an amazing writer, confidant, friend—you complete me!

XOXO

-Lee

# WANT MORE? ALPHA'S MISSION

*Please enjoy this preview of the next book in the series—Alpha's Mission*

*Charlie*

Blood in my mouth... not mine.

Tastes... so good.

*No.* Not good. Wrong.

Change back, dammit.

*Shift.*

When nothing happens, I tear up the mountainside, through the trees, leaping over fallen logs and boulders. My white paws are huge on the soft pine needles.

What's that? Movement in the bushes. I leap and twist in the air, take off after the running jackrabbit.

It doesn't stand a chance. I'm too fast. Too ferocious.

More blood fills my mouth, hot and thick. I gobble down the rabbit's flesh like a starved dog.

Then I trot down to the creek and drink from it.

When I see my reflection in the water, I bite at the big, silver and white wolf.

*Shift, you monster. Shift.*

I don't even know where the fuck I am. How to get back. My brain doesn't work right. I have no control over my body. My... urges.

I turn and trot in the direction I'm pulled and somehow, miraculously, end up in front of my truck.

The desire to get in that truck and drive off this mountain, away from what happened here is so strong, I sit and whine at the door handle.

*Shift back.*

What did Jared say to make me change back in Honduras? Just *shift back*. I cast my mind to that moment, seeing my white paws for the first time, the heat and rearranging of my cells, and suddenly, I'm on my side, naked, panting.

*Human.*

Thank fuck.

I'm human again. Eighteen hours I've been roaming this mountain trying to figure out how to change back.

Coming here and letting the monster out was a mistake. I wipe my mouth, disgusted by the taste of blood. When the memory of what I ate comes flooding back, I heave behind the car.

Christ. It's not like me to not have my own body under control. This sack of bones has been a machine for me from the moment I entered the Army and got out of Kentucky at age eighteen. I can kill with my bare hands, escape any danger. I work best under pressure.

This is no time to get sensitive.

I just can't stand feeling out of control, not knowing what I'm going to do next. The way I succumbed to the animal's need to hunt—I couldn't control it. The way the waxing moon brought me out here last night.

Shit. What time is it?

I grab the keys I hid on top of the driver's side wheel and open the truck.

Twelve-fucking-thirty. I missed a meeting with my handler. I'm so fucked.

I yank on my jeans while I call Agent Annabel Gray.

"Dune, what happened to you? You've been off the grid for twenty hours." She'd checked my tracking device. I only keep it on when I'm on an active mission.

Do I hear relief in her voice? Was Ann Gray worried about me? It's an odd thought, but my relationship with her changed last month when I asked her for help tracking the... *werewolves*. Now, I know what they are.

What *I* am.

Anyway, there's trust between us. She did me a favor, said I owe her one in return.

That piece of information has had me mulling over what I know about her. What could she possibly need from me?

"I'm sorry," I say, pulling on my shirt and getting behind the wheel. "I missed our meeting."

"Is everything okay?" There's an awkward hesitation in her voice. It *is* personal.

"I'm not hurt." That much is true. For some reason, I don't want to lie to her, and I'm definitely not okay.

Finding out I'm a werewolf—having my werewolf genes triggered or activated by seeing others of... my kind —definitely threw me for a loop. I question my sanity on a daily basis. But more importantly, I question my efficacy. My senses are in overdrive. I hear too much, smell too many scents, crave meat like I'm going to die if I don't kill something. If I can't control my animalistic urges, what's going to happen when I'm on a job? When lives are at risk?

"I spent the night... out of the city. I can meet in ninety minutes. Give me a location."

She blows out an impatient breath. "Venice Beach, 1430 hours."

"I'll find you there."

I hang up my phone and step on the gas. I don't usually give a shit about pissed off handlers. My job performance isn't graded on how well I interface with others, it's how well I complete my missions. But for some reason—maybe because she sounded like she cared—I'm in a hurry to see Agent Gray face to face.

Maybe even to apologize.

～

*Annabel*

I buy an ice cream cone and sit on the wall at Venice Beach, blending in with the hordes of beachgoers. I dressed to fit in—I'm wearing a halter top and shorts with wrap-around sandals I can run in if I need to.

I can't believe I'm upset Charlie Dune hooked up with someone last night. Why in the hell would I care?

We don't have a relationship.

I'm his handler, for God's sake.

Yeah, he's hot. All the field agents I've met appeal to me. I mean what's not enthralling about highly intelligent men whose bodies are trained weapons? Agents who supposedly can single-handedly bring down governments or start wars? Agents who can rescue hostages or—rumor has it—execute a kill order? I know I've never passed along orders like that, but my clearance level isn't high.

Dune, like all field agents, is built of chiseled muscle. He's not huge or tall, they never are. They need to be able to slip in and out of places unnoticed—blend in.

I have a thing for spies, I guess, particularly Dune. Something happened last month between us. Actually, it's probably all in my head. Which is why I'm an intelligence analyst, not a field agent—I over-emotionalize, get personal with people and situations. I care too deeply. Despite my basic combat training, I'd never be able to pull the trigger on anyone even if my life depended on it.

I bent some rules and put my own job on the line to get some information last month for Dune. He said he lost someone involved with the lab fires. And I probably over-personalized that. Because I know what it's like to investigate our government's dirty secrets when it involves a loved one.

"Chocolate—my favorite," a deep voice rumbles behind me.

I don't jump. I'm used to him appearing out of thin air. What I'm not used to is how close he comes in. If I didn't think it was crazy, I'd swear he leaned in to inhale my scent.

I turn and find his face too near to mine, and the green of his eyes appears to change to ice blue in the sunlight.

Damn.

Yeah, he's hotter than I remembered. In a tight black t-shirt—the kind that stretches over his hard muscles—and a ball cap pulled low over his green eyes, he looks the perfect hunky, California surfer.

He steals the ice cream cone from me and takes a big lick. Well, this is definitely different. We're practically sharing spit.

Is he flirting?

Oh, that's ripe. After he missed our morning meeting because of some hook-up he had. I never knew Dune was such a player, but it fits. Field agents can't have permanent relationships, so they become man-whores, getting it whenever and wherever they want.

Asshole.

I turn to face him and watch as he completely demolishes the ice cream cone. I mean, I didn't know you could eat a cone that fast.

So, I guess we're not sharing spit.

He has the grace to look shame-faced as he licks the last bit off his fingers.

"I'll buy you another one."

I roll my eyes. "Don't bother. I only bought it for cover."

"What's the assignment?"

I can't stop my annoyance from surfacing even though he's always all-business.

"Your no-show this morning may have cost us the mission."

His face remains impassive, and under the ballcap, his eyes keep roving the landscape like he's taking in every person who passes, everything about our surroundings. He's so damn *alert*.

"I'll fix it. What's the mission?"

The thing is—I believe him. I'm sure he'll fix it. He's the kind of agent who gets results which is why he gets paid the big bucks.

Still, I'm not over feeling pissy. I flick on my tablet and share the screen with him. "Target is Lucius Frangelico. He lives in Hollywood. Occupation, unknown. Possible mafia, possible drug kingpin. Definitely into something. They want him bugged and tracked."

"Why is this a CIA job rather than FBI?"

"He has ties to Al Qaeda. Travels internationally. May be selling weaponry. This is a preliminary investigation."

"I'll take care of it."

"Yeah, well, he left California this afternoon on a private plane. So, now you have to find him."

He nods, sober. "I will."

I'm sure he's right. I have complete faith in him. And I still feel like he owes me an apology for no-showing to our meeting earlier.

As if he reads minds, too, he meets my gaze. "I'm sorry about this morning. It won't happen again."

"Dune, I don't care what you do on your off-time, but when I call you in, you show up." I can pull a bitch when the occasion calls for it.

He rubs a hand across his stubbled jaw, still subtly glancing in all directions without moving his head. "Yeah. I was... incapacitated."

I arch a brow. "Was she that good?"

His head draws back, and his brows slam down. "What?" His laugh is unexpected—maybe to both of us. I detect relief in it which I file away to examine later. "No, it wasn't a woman—I wish." He gives his head a quick shake. "I mean —" He stops, his jade eyes meeting mine.

For a second neither of us speaks, gazes tangled, locked. Something flutters in my belly. His nostrils flare, and I watch the same trick of the light make his eyes flash blue. My lips part in surprise, and his gaze dips there.

"It wasn't a woman." His voice is deeper than I remember.

"What was it, then?" My voice has lost all authority—it sounds pathetically breathy to my ears.

He shakes his head. "Something else." He suddenly looks tired, almost defeated.

I'm shocked by a need to soothe him, a need to know what demons haunt this brave warrior. What does he hide under that impenetrable mask of deadly capability?

"Listen." He touches my nape, just under where the halter top ties. Energy shoots through me at the light contact, tingles of pleasure racing across my skin. I know this is just for show—we're playing the part of a flirty beach couple, but the thrumming that starts between my legs doesn't understand that. "I want to thank you for the help you gave me last month. You helped save a kidnapped child, so... it made a difference."

My mind wants to run down the path of figuring out whose child he was saving—his, a friend's—but all I can focus on is the light circles he traces on my skin. My breath hitches.

"I'm glad it helped."

"I owe you one. Call it in when you need it."

My nipples tighten. "Oh, I will." The confidence returns to my voice, but for some inexplicable reason, I choose this moment to blush. Maybe because of his penetrating stare as if he's trying to decipher what possible reason I might have for requesting a favor from him.

I hope to God I'll never need to. But the file I extracted for him isn't the only redacted data I've hacked. And considering which department of the government I work for, consequences could be more than a slap on the wrist. You never know.

So, having a friend capable of protecting my life could come in handy.

"You've uploaded the information to me?" he asks, tapping my tablet, back to business.

"Yes." I nod. "Let me know when it's done."

"Of course." He starts to step away, then turns back. "Annabel."

He's never called me by my first name before. It has an effect on me like he has me by the throat—but in a good way. He commands my full attention—my stiff nipples throb, tingles race over my skin.

"Are you in some kind of trouble?"

I hesitate, then shake my head. *Not yet.*

He nods. "You'll tell me when I need to know."

Then he's gone, blending into the crowd of people, and disappearing as quickly as he appeared.

Right. I'll tell him when he needs to know.

I truly hope that time won't come.

Why, then, does the idea of *not* sharing my secret with him disappoint me?

READ NOW

# READ ALL THE BAD BOY ALPHA BOOKS

**Bad Boy Alphas Series**
*Alpha's Temptation*
*Alpha's Danger*
*Alpha's Prize*
*Alpha's Challenge*
*Alpha's Obsession*
*Alpha's Desire*
*Alpha's War*
*Alpha's Mission*
*Alpha's Bane*
*Alpha's Secret*
*Alpha's Prey*
*Alpha's Blood*
*Alpha's Sun*

**Shifter Ops**
*Alpha's Moon*
*Alpha's Vow*
*Alpha's Revenge*

***Midnight Doms***
*Alpha's Blood*
*His Captive Mortal*
*Additional books by other authors*

# WANT FREE BOOKS?

**Go to http://subscribepage.com/alphastemp** to sign up for Renee Rose's newsletter and receive a free books. In addition to the free stories, you will also get special pricing, exclusive previews and news of new releases.

Download a free Lee Savino book from www.leesavino.com

# OTHER TITLES BY RENEE ROSE

**Paranormal**

**Bad Boy Alphas Series**

*Alpha's Temptation*

*Alpha's Danger*

*Alpha's Prize*

*Alpha's Challenge*

*Alpha's Obsession*

*Alpha's Desire*

*Alpha's War*

*Alpha's Mission*

*Alpha's Bane*

*Alpha's Secret*

*Alpha's Prey*

*Alpha's Sun*

**Shifter Ops**

*Alpha's Moon*

*Alpha's Vow*

*Alpha's Revenge*

**Wolf Ranch Series**

*Rough*

*Wild*

*Feral*

*Savage*

*Fierce*

*Ruthless*

*Untamed*

**Wolf Ridge High Series**

*Alpha Bully*

*Alpha Knight*

***Midnight Doms***

*Alpha's Blood*

*His Captive Mortal*

***Alpha Doms Series***

*The Alpha's Hunger*

*The Alpha's Promise*

*The Alpha's Punishment*

**Other Paranormal**

*The Winter Storm: An Ever After Chronicle*

**Contemporary**

**Chicago Bratva**

*"Prelude" in Black Light: Roulette War*

*The Director*

*The Fixer*

*"Owned" in Black Light: Roulette Rematch*

*The Enforcer*

**Vegas Underground Mafia Romance**

*King of Diamonds*

*Mafia Daddy*

*Jack of Spades*

*Ace of Hearts*

*Joker's Wild*

*His Queen of Clubs*

*Dead Man's Hand*

*Wild Card*

**Daddy Rules Series**

*Fire Daddy*

*Hollywood Daddy*

*Stepbrother Daddy*

*Master Me Series*

*Her Royal Master*

*Her Russian Master*

*Her Marine Master*

*Yes, Doctor*

*Double Doms Series*

*Theirs to Punish*

*Theirs to Protect*

*Holiday Feel-Good*

*Scoring with Santa*

*Saved*

*Other Contemporary*

*Black Light: Valentine Roulette*
*Black Light: Roulette Redux*
*Black Light: Celebrity Roulette*
*Black Light: Roulette War*
*Black Light: Roulette Rematch*
*Punishing Portia (written as Darling Adams)*
*The Professor's Girl*
*Safe in his Arms*

## Sci-Fi

### Zandian Masters Series

*His Human Slave*
*His Human Prisoner*
*Training His Human*
*His Human Rebel*
*His Human Vessel*
*His Mate and Master*
*Zandian Pet*
*Their Zandian Mate*
*His Human Possession*

### Zandian Brides

*Night of the Zandians*
*Bought by the Zandians*
*Mastered by the Zandians*
*Zandian Lights*
*Kept by the Zandian*
*Claimed by the Zandian*

*Stolen by the Zandian*

**Other Sci-Fi**

*The Hand of Vengeance*

*Her Alien Masters*

**Regency**

*The Darlington Incident*

*Humbled*

*The Reddington Scandal*

*The Westerfield Affair*

*Pleasing the Colonel*

**Western**

*His Little Lapis*

*The Devil of Whiskey Row*

*The Outlaw's Bride*

**Medieval**

*Mercenary*

*Medieval Discipline*

*Lords and Ladies*

*The Knight's Prisoner*

*Betrothed*

*The Knight's Seduction*

*The Conquered Brides (5 book box set)*

*Held for Ransom (out of print)*

**Renaissance**

*Renaissance Discipline*

# ALSO BY LEE SAVINO

**Paranormal romance**

The Berserker Saga and Berserker Brides (menage werewolves)

*These fierce warriors will stop at nothing to claim their mates.*

Draekons (Dragons in Exile) with Lili Zander (menage alien dragons)

*Crashed spaceship. Prison planet. Two big, hulking, bronzed aliens who turn into dragons. The best part? The dragons insist I'm their mate.*

Bad Boy Alphas with Renee Rose (bad boy werewolves)

*Never ever date a werewolf.*

Tsenturion Masters with Golden Angel

*Who knew my e-reader was a portal to another galaxy? Now I'm stuck with a fierce alien commander who wants to claim me as his own.*

**Contemporary Romance**

Royal Bad Boy

*I'm not falling in love with my arrogant, annoying, sex god boss. Nope. No way.*

Royally Fake Fiancé

*The Duke of New Arcadia has an image problem only a fiancé can fix. And I'm the lucky lady he's chosen to play Cinderella.*

Beauty & The Lumberjacks

*After this logging season, I'm giving up sex. For...reasons.*

## Her Marine Daddy

*My hot Marine hero wants me to call him daddy...*

## Her Dueling Daddies

*Two daddies are better than one.*

## Innocence: dark mafia romance with Stasia Black

*I'm the king of the criminal underworld. I always get what I want. And she is my obsession.*

## Beauty's Beast: a dark romance with Stasia Black

*Years ago, Daphne's father stole from me. Now it's time for her to pay her family's debt...with her body.*

# ABOUT RENEE ROSE

**USA TODAY BESTSELLING AUTHOR RENEE ROSE** loves a dominant, dirty-talking alpha hero! She's sold over a million copies of steamy romance with varying levels of kink. Her books have been featured in USA Today's *Happily Ever After* and *Popsugar*. Named Eroticon USA's Next Top Erotic Author in 2013, she has also won *Spunky and Sassy's* Favorite Sci-Fi and Anthology author, *The Romance Reviews* Best Historical Romance, and *has* hit the *USA Today* list seven times with her Wolf Ranch series and various anthologies.

**Please follow her on:**
   Bookbub | Goodreads

*Renee loves to connect with readers!*
www.reneeroseromance.com
reneeroseauthor@gmail.com

# ABOUT LEE SAVINO

Lee Savino is a USA today bestselling author, mom and chocoholic.

Warning: Do not read her Berserker series, or you will be addicted to the huge, dominant warriors who will stop at nothing to claim their mates.

I repeat: Do. Not. Read. The Berserker Saga. Particularly not the thrilling excerpt below.

Download a free book from www.leesavino.com (don't read that either. Too much hot, sexy lovin').